LEGBITER

David McLachlan

EBONY MUSIC & BOOKS

First published in Great Britain in 2017 by

Ebony Music & Books
10a Sandgate Court
Rainham
GILLINGHAM
ME8 8TQ

www.ebonymusic.co.uk

A CIP catalogue record for this book
is available from the British Library

ISBN 978-1546500261

To my children and grandchildren.

And my two Mums,

who brought me to Argyll in the first place.

MID ARGYLL

CONTENTS

PROLOGUE

The battle was disappointingly short. Ketil, the Norse leader, strode forward, his cloak billowing out behind him. He was a tall man, and as he jumped up onto the empty cart he towered over the scene. From his vantage point, he could see over the roofs of the small houses before him and down to the waters of the loch. Through a gap in the trees, he was able to make out the square black sail of his longship.

The houses were clustered round a large area of grass in the middle of the settlement. The defeated villagers were herded onto the green where they were soon joined by the monks from the church on the hill above. As the villagers were forced to kneel onto the ground, Ketil stole a glance at the sword still gripped in his hand. Blood was running down the length of the blade, dripping onto the floor of the cart.

These journeys to Alba were so profitable for him and the Norsemen who came with him. The settlements were poorly defended and it was a simple matter for him to take what he wanted. Staring at the sorry group of Scots in front of him he reckoned there were just over thirty. But where were the men? Hunting? Fishing? Most of the people gathered on the village green were women and children. Any men he could see were old and infirm. Defeating such a crowd was child's play.

Ketil lifted his free arm as a sign that he would address the crowd. He could see the monks in their robes excitedly trying to speak in a language unknown to the Vikings. The men guarding them under Ubbe's command kept prodding them with their spears until they finally fell silent.

Ketil had a particular dislike of Christian monks. They were supposed to be intelligent people. They could write books and paint pictures. They encouraged people to give them money, and their churches were often filled with valuables. And yet they did not fight to hold their treasure. They did not guard their wealth against robbers. In his eyes they were fools. They deserved to lose everything.

When Ketil spoke, it was to his own men. 'Search the houses and the church. Take anything of value to us. Be sure to look well in the church. Then, burn the buildings.'

Ubbe's men continued to surround the prisoners as the rest of the raiders headed into the houses and the sacred place at the top of the hill. At the same time, two men advanced slowly towards Ketil as if the searching was not a task that required them. One of them was taller than Ketil himself. He wore a cloak that added to his bulk. Beside him, his brother Runolf's hair was black as night. Beneath the curtain of hair, Runolf's eyes darted quickly around him in all directions, and his mouth was twisted into a cold sneer.

Ketil smiled as his sons approached him. The bigger man was tapping the hilt of his sword. 'What's next?' he asked, turning to look behind him at the people cowering on the ground.

'What's next?' repeated his father.

'After we burn the houses?'

Ketil thought about the journey home. He had noticed some livestock in the village but there were few enough provisions without having to feed a group of prisoners. He looked down to his sons, and spoke quietly. 'After we burn the houses … we kill!'

He made a wide sweeping movement with his arm. 'Kill everyone!' Gris and Runolf began to smile as they began to draw their swords.

That was what they wanted to hear.

THE MISSING BOAT

'Then there are the midges!'

Emma's eyes shot up quickly, staring over the top of her magazine.

'The what?' Her brow was knitted in the comical way it did whenever she was trying hard to remember something. Across from her, Ben was grinning from ear to ear. She recognised the smug face he liked to make whenever he had added something special to one of his famous lists.

'Midges are like invisible flies that come and eat your blood, and they are very annoying,' he announced proudly.

'I don't think I believe in invisible flies,' Emma said, looking at the back of her Mum's head in the hope of some reassurance. Mum kept staring ahead with her hands on the wheel but she was tuned in to the conversation.

'Ben is right, Emma. Midges are the smallest flies in Scotland, and they do sometimes bite humans, but their bite is more itchy than sore. Last time we were round here we had to put cream on you when we went out in the evening.

Don't you remember?'

Emma didn't like the sound of this. 'Well how come we don't ever have midges in Glasgow?'

'They seem to like the west coast,' said Mum. 'Maybe they just love all this beautiful scenery. Look out the window. Look at the mountains and the water. You can't see this back home!'

Their car was travelling down the shoreline of Loch Fyne, a few miles north of Lochgilphead, and the children had to admit that their surroundings were special. Each time they came to a break in the trees at the water's edge, there was a magical view of sunshine reflected on the surface of the loch and a glimpse of the purple hills stretching into the clouds. At least the weather was holding.

During the journey, Ben had been working on two lists. On the one hand, there were *some* good things about going away for a few days. He might get to scramble over the hills, or light a fire on the beach and cook a picnic. At Lochgilphead there was the putting green – if it was open, and the swimming pool – which wasn't too bad. At Aunt Isobel's house itself there wasn't much to do, but there was Colin, who lived next door, with his great stories and – best of all – his boat. Going out fishing with Colin was what Ben was looking forward to most.

On the other hand, his negative list was much longer. He didn't want to be away from his friends for two weeks; he had written down all the things he could possibly have been doing with them during that time. He didn't like the idea of his Dad not being on this trip for the first few days. Apart from anything else, there wouldn't be much fun in kicking a ball about in Aunt Isobel's back garden all by himself.

Last time he was here it had rained nearly every day and he remembered feeling bored, and cold – and that had been summer.

Ben was actually pleased to have thought of the midges; they added more doom to his list and helped convince him that he was right to believe he would be better off back home rather than sitting in the back of a car on this winding road. Mum was a good driver but the road twisted and turned continually in front of them and he was starting to feel queasy.

The thick forest on their left seemed to be coming to an end, and a wide expanse of bay opened out in front of them. At the far side they could make out houses built close to the water's edge. 'This is Loch Gair,' said Mum. 'Not long to go now.'

'I thought I saw a sign saying Asknish,' said Ben, looking across at the flat, peaceful water of the sheltered cove.

'I think Asknish is the old name for the other side of the bay. Anyway, this is where Colin usually keeps his boat.'

Ben was already scanning the water, but the trees kept blocking his view. There were only a few boats moored in the harbour but it was impossible to see any of them clearly. A seagull took off from an outcrop of rock with something in its beak, pursued by another two birds. The three gulls swooped and circled in the sky above them.

Beside Ben, Emma sat with her eyes closed, oblivious to what was happening. One hand gripped her trusty iPod; the other tapped out a rhythm on the windowpane. *Probably Beyonce, or some pathetic boy band,* thought Ben.

A few minutes later they stopped at Lochgilphead for some supplies. The tide was out completely, leaving an ugly, muddy sandbank stretching for at least a mile out to the water. The sun was still shining, and as they came out of the store, Ben noticed with relief that there were people using the putting green.

As well as bread and flowers for Aunt Isobel, there were a couple of packets of sticks wrapped in polythene – kindling for the fire. Both children remembered the coal fire at the cottage and how much fun it was to get it to light. On their last trip they had challenged each other to see who could create the best fire in the shortest time.

'How far is it to go now before we get to Aunt Isobel's?' asked Emma, once they had finished packing the car.

'It's only about another five minutes from here,' said Mum. 'She's really looking forward to seeing you two.'

The car left the main road just after the signs for Cairnbaan, and slowly climbed the gravel path towards the Achnabreck cottages. At the top of the track, halfway up the hill, three white buildings came into view and they turned into the driveway of the first house. It was a long time since a car had been in regular use here – not since Isobel's husband Hector had died. As she switched the engine off, Mum turned round to smile at the children. 'Here we are, at last. Now please be good to your aunt. She's not been having a very happy time lately.'

Technically Isobel was Mum's aunt. This meant that she was really the children's great aunt, and to them she certainly seemed old. But 'Great Aunt' was a bit of a mouthful, so to Emma and Ben she was Aunt Isobel. They knew they had come to visit just now because their Mum was worried about her aunt's health and kept saying something about being 'next of kin'.

The three buildings had whitewashed walls and dull grey roofs. Colin's house was behind the other two, near to the steep rocks of the hillside. Despite the heat of the day, wisps of smoke curled out from one of the chimneys. Next to Isobel's cottage was the second building which lay empty for much of the year as it was used as a holiday home. Yet this house had recently been re-roofed and looked in much better condition than its occupied neighbours.

Tall trees framed Isobel's cottage and a small grove of birches to one side partly shadowed the outhouse; this was used as a store and was filled with logs and coal. The window frames on the cottage itself were painted red, as was the door which began to open as soon as Emma and Ben followed their mother up the path.

The two women embraced at the doorway. 'It's so lovely to see you, Katie,' said Aunt Isobel as she reached up to hug her niece. Isobel's long silver-grey hair was tied back in a ponytail and her brown cardigan was the one she always seemed to wear. 'Look at you two!' she exclaimed. 'Emma and Ben: how old are you now?'

'I'm thirteen and Ben is eleven,' replied Emma.

'Well you've certainly grown.'

The children smiled back as they sighed inwardly. They had heard these words many times before.

* * *

'She doesn't seem too unwell to me,' said Emma. She was swinging her legs, sitting on one of the single beds in the room she was sharing with her wee brother. Ben sat across from her, carefully unpacking his rucksack.

'She does seem a bit older and slower now – though she

can still cook a good meal.' Ben agreed. They had enjoyed their dinner and Mum (of course her aunt called her *Katie*) and Isobel were now settled together in the living room, chatting over a cup of tea. A worried frown suddenly came over Ben's face. 'Do you think we'll have to eat that fish she usually makes for breakfast?'

Emma laughed. 'You mean kippers? Don't worry. I saw Corn Flakes in the kitchen.' She stood up. 'I'm going to ask Mum if I can go over to see Colin now. D'you want to come with me?' Ben nodded and pulled on a jumper.

The sun was sinking behind the hills as Emma and Ben made their way up the stony path towards Colin's house. They were beginning to adjust to the quiet of the countryside. Here there was no sound of traffic, and even Colin's house seemed to be deserted as they banged on his door. Birds calling from the trees above them broke the silence as they waited. Then there was the noise of a handle turning and Colin stood above them, his broad frame filling the doorway. 'Well if it isn't young Emma and Ben. Come away in,' he said in his lilting voice, beckoning them to enter with a sweeping movement of his giant arm.

Colin's cottage was laid out in the same shape as Aunt Isobel's, and like their aunt's house it was old fashioned – seeming to belong to another era. It even had the same damp smell as their aunt's. The children knew that the houses they were used to in Glasgow didn't smell like this; they reckoned the aroma was due to the coal fires and the countryside.

Unlike Isobel's neat and tidy home, Colin's was full of 'stuff'. Books, pamphlets and maps were everywhere. There were so many pictures that the walls could have taken no more. And there were interesting objects piled up everywhere. In fact it could be hard to find a seat in Colin's living room. Katie, the children's mum, would have said it 'lacked a woman's touch', but then Colin had lived by himself for many years. To Emma and Ben, it was like a treasure trove.

The children sat looking across at their aunt's giant neighbour. His hair was thinning but his beard was bushy and full. The old fisherman's jumper he wore seemed overly warm for a summer's evening indoors but they had rarely seen him wear anything else. His clothes were old and dirty but his eyes sparkled with fun, and he listened intently as they updated him with the news of their school, and told him of their Mum's concern for Isobel that was the main reason for their coming. Emma explained that their Dad couldn't join them for a few days because of his work.

When it seemed to Ben that enough pleasantries had been exchanged, he decided to ask the big question. 'On the way here we went past Loch Gair and we were looking at the boats. I was wondering whether, seeing as we are here for a few days, we might get a chance to go out in your boat and do some fishing together?'

To his horror, Colin began to shake his head. 'I'm sorry to tell you,' he said, 'but I sold the boat.'

Ben's heart was sinking. 'Why did you do that?'

'Well, I wasn't using it that much and I'm not getting any younger. It's quite heavy to lug about and manoeuvre. So about six months ago, I got rid of it altogether I'm afraid.'

With these few words, the very best item on Ben's list had just been crossed off. The one thing both children were really hoping to do on this trip to Achnabreck was now definitely out of the question. As the conversation continued, Colin said there would be other good things to do but Ben sat looking at the floor, struggling to accept the news. Emma wanted to say something to cheer him up but decided against it when she saw the black expression on his face. He was in no mood to consider alternatives.

* * *

The next day was clear and bright and the children appeared in the kitchen for breakfast having slept well despite their unfamiliar beds. There were no kippers waiting for them. Isobel had cooked a fry-up with sausages, bacon, eggs and potato scones. Emma hungrily wolfed it down but Ben settled for Corn Flakes. Once everyone had eaten Mum made an announcement: 'Aunt Isobel and I are going into Lochgilphead this morning to get some things. If you like, we can take you down to the swimming baths. We'll pick you up later.'

Emma loved swimming and Ben had no other plans, so they packed their bags and joined Isobel and Katie in the car. Emma reminded Ben about the grumpy old man they had encountered the last time they had gone swimming there. Both secretly hoped they might meet him again. The pool was busy because of the school holidays, and most of the other children there seemed to know each other, but there was no sign of the angry man.

When they came out of the pool, Katie and Isobel were just pulling up in the car. Mum called over to them, 'We've done all we came here to do today. But I've just met Colin in the town, and he turned down my offer of a lift. He said it's such a good day he is going to walk home along the banks of the Crinan Canal. He wondered if you two cared to join him. It *is* a lovely day.'

Ben looked doubtful. 'How can we get home along the canal?'

'You just keep going on the path until you get to Cairnbaan and cross over to the road. It should be a nice walk,' said Emma.

Katie was nodding. 'Emma's right. Jump in the car and I'll take you along to the canal lock at Oakfield Bridge. Colin will meet you there.'

Ben and Emma climbed the short incline up to the canal which, at this point, was above the level of the main road. Oakfield was more than a canal lock; it was a swing bridge that could be crossed by cars though they wondered how many cars actually made regular use of it. There was a large house at the bridge on the banks of the canal. The children sat in front of it, taking in their peaceful surroundings. Facing them on the other side of the water was a dense wood. To their left, the canal headed southwards to the village of Ardrishaig about a couple of miles away. To their right the canal twisted along towards Cairnbaan, eventually ending up at Crinan itself – about seven miles away.

The quiet was broken by a booming voice. 'Glad to see you!' Colin appeared in front of them, clambering up the slope. His thick beard did little to conceal his wide smile. 'How was your swim?'

'It was good, but the place was pretty busy,' said Emma.

'That'll be due to the school holidays I suppose. Which side do you want to walk along?'

The children hadn't considered this. A path ran along either side of the canal. 'Why don't we cross over to the other side?' suggested Ben.

As they walked across the bridge, they looked over the edge. The still water of the canal was dark. 'That water looks really deep,' said Emma, pulling herself up on the railings.

Colin patted her on the shoulder as he walked past. 'Actually, it's only about 10 feet deep.'

'Deep enough if you can't swim,' muttered Emma.

The three began walking northwards. After a couple of minutes the trees thinned out around them and they became aware of the heat on their heads. 'It's another fine day,' said Colin.

'Can you tell us one of your stories?' asked Emma.

'What kind of story had you in mind?'

'Well, you know – the stories you sometimes tell us about long ago? Tell us one of them. But make it a new one that we haven't heard before.'

'Tell us a scary story!' suggested Ben.

Colin scratched his head for a moment. Then he started to speak. 'Actually, I can tell you a scary story about where we are right now.' He pointed back over his shoulder to the thick trees at the Oakfield Bridge. The children stared behind them. 'That area used to be known as Kilduskland. Many years ago there was a monastery there. The people who lived there were called white friars. No one really knows what happened to them, but over the years, there have been rumours of sightings.'

'What does 'sightings' mean?' asked Ben.

'Ghosts! People claim to have seen ghosts here – the ghostly figures of monks.'

A gust of wind hit the three walkers as they rounded a bend in the canal. The protection from bushes and trees was all but gone here. Emma pushed her long hair away from her face. Then she looked up at the man. 'Is that true? Are there really ghosts?'

Colin tried to look very serious. 'Well I can't vouch for the existence of ghosts but these stories have certainly been told. I'm not making that up.'

Ben looked over at his sister. 'Cool!'

She grinned back at him.

THE MAGNET

The next day was dull and grey and it was raining heavily. The wind howled outside the cottage. It was hard to believe that the day before had been so pleasant. Mum was standing at the window shaking her head and gazing out at the bleak scene. 'Oh well, summertime in Argyll....'

Ben grunted agreement. Poor weather had been an important entry on his negative list. It wouldn't be so bad if there were Sky TV or decent reception for his mobile phone. Around the house there was little entertainment. He knew there was an old chess set somewhere in the cottage but Dad wasn't here to play it with him. Aunt Isobel and Emma didn't play at all and Mum hardly played – she kept talking about 'horses' instead of 'knights'.

In the children's bedroom, Ben's clothes lay neatly on the bedside table beside his pens and notebooks. Ben considered creating a new list of things that couldn't be done at Achnabreck cottage on a wet day, but realised it would just make him feel worse. Meanwhile, Emma was in there with strict instructions to do something about her clothes which were already strewn all over the floor. Tidiness didn't come easily to her and she sat on her bed stuffing fistfuls of clothes into a canvas holdall.

It was a surprise when Mum announced that she was going out with Aunt Isobel. 'We're going to take the car and visit Mary McLean in Ardrishaig. She's one of Aunt Isobel's oldest friends. They're both getting on a bit, and they don't get a chance to see each other much these days. We shouldn't be gone more than a couple of hours.'

'Okay,' replied Ben, wandering into the hallway. He was trying hard to think of somewhere he could ask to be taken to but he couldn't come up with anything. The swimming pool would be mobbed. And they had only just been there yesterday.

As his Mum passed him, she ruffled his tousled hair. 'Keep an eye on Emma. Make sure she tidies that room. And while we are away, could you tell her to go over to the outhouse and bring in some logs for the fire?'

Emma's eyes brightened. She was picturing the axe that hung on the wall of the outhouse. She called out, 'Do you want me to chop some wood?'

Isobel appeared in the room, buttoning her coat. 'Don't worry dear. There are already plenty of logs in the shed. Colin is so good at cutting them up for me.'

'Okay Aunt Isobel,' said Emma, trying hard to hide her disappointment.

After watching the car slowly descend the rough path towards the main road, she turned her attention to the outhouse. With its whitewashed walls and tiny windows, it was like a mini replica of the cottage itself The windows appeared black, giving no hint of what was inside, and they were covered with cobwebs.

The door was bolted and secured by a padlock. As Emma unlocked the door and pushed it open, she reckoned the padlock had been renewed since her last visit. Once inside, however, nothing seemed new. All appeared grey, reflecting the colour of the stone floor and walls. It was as if everything had been washed over with a coat of powdery dust. A little light came from the window beside the doorway and a small skylight in the roof. The darkness of the outhouse even in broad daylight always amazed Emma. In fact she was always a little afraid of being here on her own though she would never have admitted it.

At one time there had been two rooms, but a wall had been knocked down on the far side. Now, in what would have been the smaller room were the logs – stacked up in a solid pile, ready for the fire. Some of them gleamed yellow and gold where they had been sliced open by Colin's axe, whilst others appeared dark green and were covered with moss. Underneath the logs were small pieces of coal, remnants from where it used to be dumped. Nowadays the coal was deposited in a metal bin in the garden.

As her eyes adjusted to the darkness, Emma took in the rest of her surroundings. There were a couple of old wooden chests, some folding chairs, mops, brushes, bottles of all kinds, tins of paint and cans of oil. There was a selection of tools – most of them rusting – hanging from hooks high on the wall. On the floor, Emma could see a toaster which did not look so old.

But the biggest feature of the place was the cold. A dark

opening on one wall showed where the fireplace would have been. A building this size would be easy to heat, but somehow Emma found it hard to imagine that this place had ever been warm, or that people had once lived here.

The door handle turned abruptly, and the noise set Emma's heart racing. She could feel her mouth dry up as she spun around towards the source of the sound.

'It's me,' announced Ben. 'You look funny. Are you alright?'

'Yeah. Of course,' said Emma, letting out a deep breath. 'Just getting some logs.'

Ben started to rummage while Emma made some trips back and forward to the cottage.

'What do you call these hooks?' Ben was standing on the corner looking at a couple of fishing rods propped up against the wall. They looked as if they had seen better days. He stretched out to Emma. In his hand was a small silver object.

'That's a spinner,' she said. 'We won't be needing any fishing stuff now. Anyway, it's all rusty. No self-respecting fish would get itself caught on *this* hook.'

As Ben took the spinner from his sister and replaced it on the shelf next to the rods, he noticed a small picture partly covered by a box of matches. Picking it up, he realised it was an old fridge magnet. 'Hey, this is interesting. Come and look at this.'

Emma came over to stand at his side. 'It's just a picture of a ship. It looks like a Viking longship.'

'But look at the bottom of the ship. That isn't water.'

'What do you mean?'

'Well, it looks like there are logs under the ship – like giant tree trunks.'

Emma leaned closer to get a better view. 'You're right. Why would there be trees under a boat?'

Ben kept staring at the picture. Above the ship there were two words: 'An Tairbeart.' 'What do you think that means?' he asked.

'I've got no idea. But I think we both know someone who might help us.'

* * *

Colin handed the picture back to Ben and sat down on his usual chair. 'You don't know the story behind this?'

'Well, no. That's why we're here,' said Emma.

'An Tairbeart is the old Gaelic name for Tarbert. It's a wee village about fifteen miles from here.'

'I know that place,' said Emma. Dad's taken me there a couple of times. We took rods and fished from the pier.' She looked over at Ben. 'I don't know if you were ever there. You were a lot younger then.'

Ben shrugged his shoulders as Colin continued. 'The picture is depicting an event that happened way back in the year 1098. It's all about Magnus Barefoot.'

Emma's eyes shot up immediately.

'Are you serious?' she asked.

'It's true,' said Colin. 'That is what he was called. At that time he was the King of Norway and had conquered much of the west coast of Scotland. He was at war with the Scottish king – a man called Edgar. The two kings decided on a peace deal – Norway could have the islands and Scotland the mainland.'

'Why did Edgar give him *any* of our land?' asked Ben indignantly.

Colin smiled at him. 'In those days, Scotland was a very young country and smaller than it is today. In fact it wasn't even called Scotland. It was known in Gaelic as Alba. The first kings of Alba were struggling to rule the whole land so this seemed like a good deal to King Edgar. But Magnus cheated! He asked Edgar to define what he meant by an island and Edgar said it was anything Magnus could sail his boat around.

Magnus was keen on gaining the whole of Kintyre and the only thing that keeps it from being an island is a narrow strip of land about a mile wide – that's where Tarbert is. So he got his men to pull his ship across from the west coast to the east and claimed the whole of Kintyre for himself. They laid down giant logs and dragged the boat across the ground.'

Colin took the children over to a map that hung on his wall and showed them the area. 'Kintyre looks like a large area of land, but in the north, the water of the West Loch nearly cuts completely through it, almost reaching Loch Fyne on the other side. And there is Tarbert right there between the two lochs,' continued Colin, pointing on the map.

'But this is a *Viking* longship,' said Emma.

'That's right. Magnus was a Viking. The people of Norway were known as the Norsemen – the Vikings!'

'This is amazing!' said Emma. 'You mean the Vikings were really here – just a few miles south of here!'

'Listen,' said Colin, 'if some of the legends are true, the Vikings were all over the land around us right here in Knapdale.'

* * *

After tea, Katie noticed Ben sitting at the living room table making up one of his lists. This time Emma was by his shoulder, looking on. 'What are you two up to?' Mum asked.

Emma stood up to reply as Ben kept on working. 'Ben's writing down some of the places we want to go and visit. We had a great conversation with Colin today and he's given us lots of ideas. There are prehistoric standing stones a few miles from here. And we want to go to Dunadd and Kilmartin. Will you take us? 'They're not far away.'

'I'm sure I could do that, if that's what you want to do.'

'Mum, did you know that the Vikings were here? I thought they only came to the very north of Scotland, but Colin says they may even have been right here in Achnabreck.'

Katie smiled down at her daughter. 'Well now, Emma,' she said, 'that was a very long time ago.'

JOURNEY

It was still early when Cuan leaned over to the motionless body at his side. Gently at first, and then more vigorously, he started to shake the boy awake. 'It's time to get up. We need to move soon.'

Fiachra sat up suddenly, rubbing his eyes. All he could see around him were trees. It was still dark. Cuan stood up on the forest floor, stretched his arms above his head and yawned loudly. Then he offered Fiachra a chunk of bread. As the boy bit into the crust, Cuan started to load their horse in readiness for the journey ahead. He pulled the sword from the ground beside them and fastened it to the animal, making sure it was within easy reach. It was a necessary precaution for travellers. Then he looked back towards his son. 'Remember, we've got a long journey ahead of us today.'

Fiachra nodded. He felt a bit stiff and sore but he *was* remembering and looking forward to today. 'Can we stop for a bit when we get to Asknish?'

A trace of a smile flashed across Cuan's face. 'Well, we will have to stop somewhere. But why Asknish?'

'I really like that place,' said Fiachra.

'You really like Mor!' laughed his father.

Fiachra felt his face go red. 'Don't worry', said Cuan, stretching out his hand and pulling Fiachra onto his feet. 'I'm hoping I can sell one of my belts to her father. Maybe even a pair of shoes. So we've got some proper business there.'

As they left the cover of the trees and headed in the direction of the loch, Cuan's eyes scanned the wide expanse of sky above them. There was little colour to be seen and no sign of the sun. But the day was still young, and he felt sure it would be bright and warm. Fiachra trudged along behind him, leading the horse with its precious cargo. Many months of careful craftsmanship on Cuan's part were now sitting on the back of this animal.

Cuan was a leather worker; the load they carried with them that day mostly contained belts and pouches destined for the market at Inverary. There were some shoes too, for although Cuan had not been properly apprenticed as a shoemaker, he had discovered he had an aptitude for making them. They seemed to sell well, not only in the markets, but also in the villages and settlements they passed on their journeys.

The two travellers were used to the road especially since the unexpected death of Fiachra's mother only a year before. Cuan found himself restless and unwilling to spend much time at the family home in Ederline. These days he was always looking for a reason to be on the move and was happy trying to find customers, rather than waiting on them to seek him out. Fiachra was his only child; at fourteen years old, he had already been accompanying his father on his travels for about six years.

As he walked along with the reins in his hands, Fiachra looked ahead to the big figure striding in front of him. A curtain of dark hair splayed across Cuan's back and a sharp knife was visible in his belt. Fiachra always felt safe when he was with his father, even when they were in a potentially dangerous situation like today when they were carrying a load of valuables through mostly uninhabited countryside.

Suddenly, Cuan stopped dead in his tracks. Turning to Fiachra, he pointed to his right. 'There … between the trees. Do you see it?'

Fiachra lifted his hands to his eyes and he stared through the woods. Then a broad smile broke out on his face. 'It's the loch. We are making good time.'

Cuan kicked away a stone at his feet and continued walking along the path. 'With any luck we'll make Asknish by noon.' As he followed on behind him, Fiachra was lost in thought. He was thinking about his mother and how he missed her; he knew that his father also still struggled with the pain of separation. Then he began remembering previous adventures on the road. Before long he was once again revisiting in his mind that unforgettable day two years ago.

It had been another trip with his father – this time to Kintyre. They had only just reached the very north of that district and were descending the hill to the village of Tairbeart when riders came into view. The riders were pushing their horses hard despite the steep incline – obviously men in a hurry. By their attire it was clear that they were not local people; the leaders in the group were finely dressed with leather boots and fur trims adorning their cloaks. Behind them rode a small detachment of soldiers in chainmail, brandishing spears and shields.

Cuan grabbed Fiachra and pulled him away from the track. He continued to keep a firm grip on his son as the men approached. 'They are in a hurry. Let them go past'.

As they drew near, Fiachra stared at the appearance of the riders. It was rare to see people dressed in such finery. But these men seemed ill at ease, and were shouting at each other. Fiachra heard only a snippet of conversation.

'We should not leave here so soon.' The words were directed at the first rider.

As the gallop continued, and the horses stumbled over the loose stones on the road, the leader swung round in his saddle to reply. 'We have seen enough! The King needs our report.'

With that, the riders in their finery and the group of supporting soldiers were gone. Cuan and Fiachra stepped back onto the path to continue their descent. They were puzzling over what they had just witnessed. But what they saw at the bottom of the hill was something they would never forget.

Tairbeart was built around a natural harbour and the water of Loch Fyne swept into the shore. A cluster of small houses nestled around the bay, with one larger building, which served as an inn, dominating the village. A surprisingly large crowd had gathered at the water's edge, including some in yet stranger attire. But each one of them was looking away from the loch. As Cuan and Fiachra came down the path, the bulk of the hill on their side prevented them from seeing what was commanding everyone's attention.

When they reached the bottom of the hill and looked to the right, following the gaze of the crowd, their eyes opened wide in amazement. A boat was coming straight towards them across the land! It was a Viking longship in full sail and it was moving. Fiachra's mouth hung open and he blinked twice, wondering if he were going mad.

Beneath the sail could be seen a warrior in a silver helmet standing proudly at the helm, occasionally shouting things that Cuan and Fiachra could not understand. A huge number of Norsemen preceded the boat, pulling and straining at thick ropes. As he continued to stare at the scene, Fiachra saw huge logs underneath the ship. There was a constant sound of wood splintering, but though the logs creaked loudly and turned slowly, they were propelling the vessel forwards.

Some of the Vikings walked alongside, patrolling the flanks with their distinctive round shields, making sure that the native villagers kept their distance. Others held axes in their hands. It was obvious that many trees had been felled, not just to obtain logs, but also to clear a pathway for the boat to travel. Cuan tugged at the shoulder of the nearest man. 'What is happening here?'

'This is Magnus Barefoot,' he replied, 'the King of Norway. He's gone and dragged his boat across from the west loch. He aims to make this land his own and the lands to the south.'

Fiachra looked up at his father and their eyes met. 'How does that work?' asked Cuan.

The villager turned to face him. 'He's done a deal with

King Edgar. Anything he can sail around he gets to keep. He is going to claim the whole of Kintyre now for Norway. He'll say it is an island.'

Cuan shook his head. 'The King of Alba will never agree to that.'

The man standing beside him snorted and spat on the ground. 'I think he will. Edgar doesn't seem able to control the country. Anyway, his men have already given in and accepted it.' The villager pointed up the hill to where the riders had passed Cuan and Fiachra.

'We saw those men a few minutes ago,' admitted Cuan. As they looked behind the moving ship there seemed to be an endless horde of Norsemen following on behind. The west loch was out of sight, but only a mile away. The villager pointed in the direction of the loch. 'We've heard that there are at least thirty longships at anchor over there.'

The crowd was forced backwards by the Norse warriors to make room for the large ship as it rolled down to the edge of the loch and entered the water. Their roars filled the air as the hull took to the sea and was lifted up by the waves above the logs below. The large-framed man in the ship raised his arms in triumph and bellowed to the waiting crowd. The Norsemen continued to shout and cheer as their king addressed them, but the people of Tairbeart had no way of understanding the meaning of the words.

Then there was silence and one of the Vikings strode forward to the water's edge. He turned to address the local onlookers. 'Today King Magnus Olafsson, the High King, claims as his own the lands of Kintyre. Let it be known that this place is under the rule and authority of the crown of Norway. According to the agreement reached with King

Edgar, King Magnus is now king of the island of Kintyre. May there now be peace.'

The Norseman was speaking in Gaelic, and this time it was the turn of the Scots to understand what was being said, even though the words filled them with fear and uncertainty.

Fiachra stood transfixed, looking out at the impressive figure on the ship. The King's golden hair spilled out from underneath a shining helmet and his mighty beard was braided. A dark red cloak hung from his shoulders, held in place by an ornate silver pin. The movement of the wind around him caused the heavy material to billow out, revealing the metal breastplate beneath.

Magnus was grinning broadly, evidently pleased with his moment of triumph, but Fiachra's eyes rested on the huge sword hanging by his side, encased in a jewelled scabbard. The sunlight seemed drawn to the weapon as it glistened in the reflected light. Without looking round at his father, he said, 'Look at the King's sword.'

Cuan's hand rested on his son's shoulder. 'I have heard of it before. The sword is well known. It even has a name. They call it *Legbiter*. That sword has killed many men.' Fiachra shivered, still staring at the man in the longship.

Then his father was tapping him on the back. 'Come now, Fiachra. I don't like what is happening here today. It's not safe to stay around this place. We need to go back the way we came.' So they climbed the hill northwards, leaving Tairbeart behind them. And they never returned.

Fiachra shook off the memory just as they arrived at the village of Asknish. As Cuan had predicted, it was around noon. The small settlement lay mostly on the southern side of the wide sweeping bay and there was the welcome smell of small fires and cooking to greet them.

They were not the first visitors of the day. Breccan had been there from first light. The friar made it his aim to be a frequent visitor to all the villages and hamlets on the banks of the Fyne. Like Cuan, he was always on the move. He spoke to all the residents, young or old, gave them sound advice when invited and he enjoyed the respect of everyone. This was no great surprise. After all, he was a man of God; he dealt in salvation and taught the new Christian faith. He had the reputation of being a healer, and he could read and write.

Fortunately, he also possessed a humble and kind spirit. Fiachra was very fond of him. They had often met on their travels. Sometimes Breccan, Fiachra and Cuan had journeyed together along the side of the loch and inland to the Glens at Kilbride and Kilmichael where there were already thriving churches. Fiachra loved and respected his father, who was rugged and strong and once served as a soldier. But he was also drawn towards the gentleness of Breccan and impressed by the sense of peace he seemed to carry with him.

Already that morning Breccan had gathered the villagers together for a service in the small chapel that was being built on the northern shores of the bay. It was taking a long time to complete, partly because the men of the village were only able to help with the construction in their spare time, and partly because it was, on Breccan's instructions, being built out of stone. The monk told the people of Asknish that when the structure was complete, it would be dedicated to St Bride – though few of them knew much about the saint they were to honour.

Breccan was saying his farewells and getting ready to

begin a new journey as Fiachra and Cuan arrived. The two travellers embraced the monk.

'It's good to see you, Brother Breccan.'

'And you, Cuan. And Fiachra, how are you?'

'I'm well enough,' replied the boy.

'Where are you heading?'

'We are going north to the market at Inverary,' said Fiachra.

'I thought you might be going there. Well, I am heading south.'

'Will you stay and eat with us?'

'That would be good,' admitted the monk, 'But I'm afraid I've been here all day already, and I need to be moving on.' He gripped Cuan's arm and Fiachra's shoulder with his hands. 'May God go with you.'

'God go with you,' they replied, and stood for a moment watching the monk start out into the trees.

ATTACK!

As Fiachra finished tethering the horse, Cuan reached into the bags slung over the animal's back. Despite the large quantity of items, Cuan soon found what he was looking for. He quickly produced three leather belts which he threw across his shoulder as he walked. 'Let's see what Preddan thinks of my belts,' Cuan said, and motioned for Fiachra to follow.

Preddan was standing at the doorway to his house when he saw the two approach. He smiled towards them as they drew near. Fiachra looked at the folds on Preddan's tunic and noticed that only a length of rope was holding the cloth together. It looked as if selling a belt to this man was a real possibility!

When they reached the house, Preddan invited them inside. It was cool and dark despite the midday sunshine outside. On one side, there was a rustling sound from the pigs moving about in their pen, but there were no other humans. Fiachra was disappointed. 'Orlaith isn't here just now. She is up at her sister's in Loch Glashan. But she should be back soon, I'd say within the hour, and she'll make us all food.'

Cuan nodded. Preddan saw that Fiachra was getting ready to speak. He predicted his question. 'Mor is with her.' Then he turned to Cuan. 'I see you've brought me some belts.' Before the men settled down to their business, Fiachra announced. 'I'm going outside for a bit. I'll be in my usual place on the rocks.' Cuan grunted approval as his son went out into the light.

It didn't take long for Fiachra to scale the small craggy hill on the southern shore of the bay. Around him were patches of grass and gorse but most of the terrain was exposed rock. From the top of the mound it was possible to see for miles in either direction across Loch Fyne. The purple hills of Glendaruel on the other side of the loch gleamed in the sunlight.

Once he had gazed around the coastline and examined the village from his new vantage point, he stole a glance at the tall wooded hills behind him. Loch Glashan lay up there in the hills. It was a small community though the loch itself was a fair size. Few people knew it existed because the traveller's path stuck close to the coastline. The settlement was built on a small island on the loch and there was a crannog (an island constructed by human hands) which contained workshops, livestock and a few houses. There was no movement from the trees. Fiachra lay down on his back and enjoyed the feeling of sun on his face.

'Fiachra! Fiachra!'

As he sat up, he could see the girl waving to him from the

sand below. Fiachra raised his arm in reply and watched in delight as she started to scale the rocks towards him, jumping and scrambling over the heather. Already he could see that she was wearing the soft boots that Cuan had given her on their last visit here. Her dress was plain and dark, contrasting with her fair skin and her hair was a mass of long black curls. As she reached the top and joined him, he saw at last the sparkle in her eyes.

'It's so good to see you, Mor,' said Fiachra.

'And you,' panted Mor, falling down breathlessly beside him.

'How long are you here for?' she asked.

'Only an hour or so,' replied Fiachra. 'We are on our way to the market up in Inverary. My father has a lot of things to sell, so we can't stay long.'

'That's a pity. But you *are* staying for some food? Mother is making a meal for us all to share.'

'I'm looking forward to that! Orlaith is a good cook,' said Fiachra.

'It's so lovely up here,' said Mor. She lay back on the grass.

Fiachra looked down on Mor, her dark hair framing her head. He wanted to kiss her. He had never kissed a girl before. But then he had never been interested in other girls. If he were ever to kiss someone, he thought, it would be Mor.

'So your aunt lives up at Loch Glashan?'

'Have you never been?' she said, sitting up.

'I've been a few times with my father. He speaks to the craftsmen up there. Some of them live in the crannog on the loch.'

'The crannog is where my aunt lives.'

'It must be interesting to live on an island.'

Mor made no reply to his comment.. Instead Fiachra noticed her expression change. She seemed to be looking beyond him.

'What is *that* on the loch?'

Fiachra turned and looked southwards. A boat was heading in their direction. It was travelling quickly and looked unfamiliarly large – certainly bigger than any of the local boats. As it slid at speed though the water, they could see oars moving rhythmically on either side and a large square sail. Mor spoke again. 'Fiachra, remember that story you told me about the day you were at Tairbeart and saw all these ships...?'

'I was just thinking about that again this morning,' interrupted Fiachra, rising quickly to his feet. 'Come with me. We need to tell everyone. That looks like a Viking ship! Fiachra pulled Mor to her feet and led the way as they began scrambling and jumping down from the rocks.

'It's a Viking ship alright.' Preddan, Cuan and a villager called Artan were standing on the rocks of Arknish Bay at the very edge of the loch. They had asked Fiachra and Mor to retreat some distance and they now stood near to the villagers who were all staring at the three men at the furthest point of the bay.

'Are you sure they have come here to attack us?' Artan asked his two companions. Everyone knew that there were peaceful Norse settlements throughout the west coast and islands of the country.

Preddan replied, 'We may not be sure, but we better be safe. We cannot risk being wrong.' Then he nodded to Artan who lifted a horn to his lips. The sound floated across the bay and brought the desired response. The men on the shore began to arm themselves.

Preddan turned to Cuan. 'We are not rich people, but we have some valuables in our village that we do not want to lose. Will you tell your son to go with Mor and hide them?'

'The valuables are in the church?'

'No. But that's where these Norsemen will look first. Mor knows where they are and where they need to go now. Tell Fiachra to go with her.'

Cuan started running back towards the village, vaulting over rocks and occasionally splashing through salt water as he went. When he reached Fiachra and Mor he told them what Preddan had asked. 'I want to stay here and fight,' said Fiachra. 'You have shown me how to handle a sword.'

'This is no time for arguing. There may be no fighting. We do not know what is going to happen but the people of Arknish need their valuables hidden. Just stay with Mor.' Then Cuan added, 'I didn't think that staying with Mor would be something that you would object to.'

Fiachra felt his arm being violently tugged. 'Come on,' said Mor, 'I know what to do.' She waved over to Orlaith who was watching her daughter anxiously from the doorway of their home. 'I'll be back soon!'

Mor led the way across the sand to a small house at the edge of the woods. It was the building furthest away from the chapel. The door was shut over, but Mor ran round behind the dwelling. At the back of the house she fell to her knees and began pulling up a heavy stone. Beneath lay a bundle of objects wrapped in a woollen cloth. Contained in the wrapping were cups and a small cross for the church, brooches, necklaces and a few coins. Breccan had made a careful list of the owners of the possessions. As Fiachra bent over and tried to scoop up the package, he had no idea of its contents. All he knew was that it was surprisingly awkward to lift.

'Now follow me,' panted Mor, and darted off into the trees.

'What *is* all this?' asked Fiachra.

But Mor was away ahead of him, gasping for breath as she climbed. It was not long before Fiachra found that he too was losing breath. The bundle of treasure in his arms was heavy, and the ground was rising fast beneath his feet. Mor was leading the way up a steep hill behind the road, as sure-footed as ever, negotiating a path between the thick trees around them. At least *she* seemed to knew where she was going.

As they ran, Mor and Fiachra could hear loud shouting, but it was impossible to see anything behind them. Fiachra's mouth was completely dry; he wondered what Mor must be feeling and thinking as she scaled the slopes in front of him.

The tree line ended, and they were out in the open. The terrain was very much like the small hill by the edge of the bay. There were steep banks of heather and a good deal of barren rock. Fiachra stopped to look down behind them. He could see the entrance to the bay, but the trees still obscured his view of the village below. As he watched, the long boat was manoeuvring itself into the harbour. It was unmistakably a Norse ship and the mainsail on the ship seemed to be black. Viking longships were built with a shallow hull which granted extra speed and allowed them to operate in very shallow water. It also meant that this ship would have no difficulty in landing on the beach itself. Fiachra couldn't make out the men below him in detail, but he could see that they were armed and hostile.

'Here! Bring it here.' Mor's anxious voice was only a few feet away. She too had stopped running; she had located the flat rock she had been seeking. Moving over to join her, Fiachra saw that, underneath the rock, a small hole had been cut out of the ground. 'This is the place,' said Mor breathlessly as Fiachra crouched down and pushed the hoard in the cloth into the earth. As the stone was dropped over the opening the secret seemed assured. There was nothing to give away the hiding place.

Fiachra and Mor sat down to get their breath. It was then that they heard shouts echoing from below them. A kind of strange singing or chanting wafted up to them – nothing Fiachra had ever heard before, not even that day in Tairbeart. Then, mingled with the shouting, were the sounds of clashing steel. A battle had commenced.

Fiachra turned to Mor. 'We can't stay here. We need to get down there. This time you follow me – but we'll go slowly.'

As Fiachra began a slow descent into the trees, Mor stood behind him in hesitation. 'What are you going to do? You don't even have a weapon.'

He beckoned her to follow. 'Don't worry, Mor. Just follow me. Trust me. I know what to do.' The words just seemed to spill from his lips.

As the girl started down the slope behind him, Fiachra considered his position. He was unarmed. He had no sense of what was happening in the village. His heart was beating wildly in his chest and he had never felt so afraid. Truthfully he had no idea what to do next.

About halfway down the hill there was a clearing in the trees. Fiachra made his way across to it, with Mor following close at his heels. But as he reached the edge of the trees, he spun quickly round to Mor. 'Stop! Right there. Don't come over here.' He was just able to utter the words before he felt his stomach heave. What he was seeing was truly sickening.

The battle was over already and the people of Asknish had been slaughtered. He could make out the body of his own father lying on the beach. Preddan lay close by. He could not see any sign of Orlaith but he knew she would not be far away. It was clear that no one had escaped. The warriors from the ship were still holding their weapons while they made their way through the village, looking for things to steal. A raiding party like this would take no prisoners. A few Norsemen lay motionless on the ground, but there was no doubt who had won the contest.

Fiachra looked across at Mor. She had listened to his instruction and had not crept to the edge of the wood. 'What's happening there? Tell me, what can you see?'

Fiachra moved back towards Mor. His body was shaking and he wondered if he could speak without being sick. At least he knew now, in the middle of this horror, what to do. They both needed to get away from here before they were seen. 'It's not good, Mor.'

A loud scream pierced the air. As Fiachra looked down, he realised that the nightmare had just got worse. Someone had seen him. Now three Norsemen were heading up the hill towards him. They were wearing leather armour and the silver on their helmets glinted through the trees as they ran.

Once again Fiachra pulled Mor to her feet. 'Someone is

coming after us. There's no time to lose.' As they ran upwards, Fiachra came up with an idea. 'Remember where we were a moment ago – just by the rocks, where there was the big patch of heather?'

'What about it?'

'We need to go there. Lead the way'.

'Will you tell me what's going on?' Mor sounded panicked.

'I'll tell you in a minute.'

They scrambled up above the tree line and Mor led the two of them to where there was a steep bank of heather and gorse bushes.

'Crawl in there and lie down flat. Don't come out until I come back for you.'

Now Mor was shrieking. 'What will *you* do?'

'Don't worry about me. I'll head them off in another direction. And then I'll be back.'

Mor opened her mouth to protest but Fiachra pushed her over into the heather. 'Get in there,' he hissed. Mor fell face down in the undergrowth. Pushing herself upwards quickly she twisted her body around, and tried to speak, but Fiachra was already gone.

The noises on the hill were getting louder as the Norsemen drew nearer. This was the most dangerous part of the plan. Fiachra wanted them to see him, and then he had to escape in another direction.

He stood waiting on a flat slab of rock. His arms were shaking as his hands clenched tightly round two small rocks. His eyes narrowed to slits as he peered into the trees below him. Suddenly the running figures materialised in the darkness below. Fiachra took aim and hurled the first of the rocks. It missed its intended target, but the men looked up to where he stood and started shouting. The second rock hurtled through the air and hit one of the Norsemen on the shoulder. He stumbled and cursed but continued on his way.

Fiachra took off up the incline behind him. Soon he was nearly at the top of the hill. Now it was time to find his way down the other side. He was exhausted, breathing heavily, but confident that he could outrun the older men. Then, at the brow of the hill, the rocks stopped abruptly and he came to a standstill just in time. The gravel under his feet flew off into space. There was a sheer drop in front of him, and the ground lay hundreds of feet below. Fiachra realised that he was trapped on this shelf of rock. There was no way forward, and behind him were his pursuers.

Just as he sensed his doom, the three men came into view. Fiachra had no idea what they were saying but he could see they were disappointed that their trail had led to such a young victim. One of the men gestured to the others to stay back. He moved forward onto the rock on which Fiachra stood, his back to the drop. The man held an axe and as he started moving towards the boy, he swung the blade in wide arcs, pushing Fiachra further and further back until he could feel his heels at the edge of the precipice.

So many thoughts crowded into Fiachra's mind. He saw his father lying dead on the sand, he thought again about his mother, and he wondered whether, even now, Mor might still escape from this tragedy. He realised that he was going to die. Perspiration ran into his eyes as he tried to focus on the ruthless killer in front of him. He thought about Breccan, and wondered if the priest was right when he said that people were reunited after death.

Then just for a moment the Norseman seemed to stumble, as if he had overreached with his weapon. There was nothing to lose. In desperation and with a blind fury, Fiachra pitched forward onto him, clawing at his face with his hands. The Viking dropped the axe, lost his balance and the youth and the man rolled over together on the rock. As the bodies separated, Fiachra was first to reach the axe.

Now it was the Norseman who was nearer the edge of the rock shelf and as he struggled to his feet, the boy sent the axe spinning round onto his attacker's foot. The man howled in pain as Fiachra's foot kicked out at his standing leg. With a piercing wail, the man pitched over the edge of the cliff, dropping to the earth below with a loud crash.

Fiachra was left standing with the weapon in his hand. He turned to face the others, but he didn't even see them. All he saw was a black shape hurtling towards him. There was a mighty crack above his eyes – the sound of his head splitting. Then darkness.

DISCOVERY

Thanks to Colin's suggestions, Ben and Emma found that a new world was opening up for them on their holiday. They'd had no idea how much history lay hidden underneath their feet. Only a few miles north of Isobel's cottage stood the prehistoric sites and monuments of Kilmartin Glen and, to their astonishment, just a few hundred yards away were two enormous slabs of rock covered with strange markings. Colin had walked them to the site and pointed out the different stars, spirals, circles and hollows carved into the surface of the stone. Ben and Emma were intrigued by what they saw. But this was only the beginning.

Over the next days they clambered with Colin across ancient rock cairns, descended into burial chambers, crossed fields to see giant standing stones at close range, and visited the atmospheric Temple Wood with its mysterious stone circles. One wet morning he took them to the museum at Kilmartin House, then next door to look at the stone crosses and burial slabs in the churchyard.

On another day, Katie took Emma to Oban to have a 'girls' day' exploring the shops together while Ben jumped into Colin's ramshackle car to drive to the ruined fortress of Dunadd. The older man told him that this place had been the capital of Dalriada – the original kingdom of the Scots before even Scotland itself had been formed.

On the top of the small hill were carvings cut into the rock, including a wild boar and a footprint. Ben stared down at the trainers he was wearing and inserted one of his feet in the hollow. It seemed to him that either his foot had grown, or the early Scots were a much smaller people. As he was reflecting on this, Colin explained that the first recorded coronation on British soil had taken place on this very spot in the 6th century, presided over by a monk called St Columba. Ben looked up quickly at the sound of that name.

'We've heard about him at our school,' he announced proudly.

* * *

One thing Emma was enjoying about this trip was having the opportunity to spend more relaxed time with her Mum. Although Katie had come to Argyll feeling anxious about her Aunt, she was much less busy and preoccupied than usual. And it seemed as if her concerns about Isobel and the rumours of breathlessness were unfounded.

Everything changed early one morning when the children were shaken roughly awake. 'Get up! Get up.' Katie's voice was insistent. Emma opened one eye cautiously. But Ben was already climbing out of bed.

'What's the matter, Mum? What time is it?' he asked.

'It's Aunt Isobel. She doesn't seem good at all. She doesn't seem to be able to breathe properly.' Katie turned to the other bed. 'Come on, Emma!' Emma threw back the covers and swung her legs out into the air. Katie took her hand and pulled her off the bed. Emma fumbled with her clothes.

'What are we going to do?'

'I'm going to have to take her to the hospital.'

'Where's the hospital?' asked Ben.

'There's one in Lochgilphead. It's not far away.'

'What's going to happen to us?'

Katie thought for a moment. 'You'll just need to come too. Unless Colin is free to look after you. I'm going up there now to ask him to help lift Aunt Isobel into the car. You kids get ready anyway!'

Emma and Ben watched as Isobel was helped into the front seat of their mother's car. The old woman sat there forlornly, head bowed, her complexion as grey as her hair. Looking on, the children felt sorry for her – she really looked so ill. 'I wish Dad were here with us all,' said Emma to no-one in particular.

Colin was talking to Katie, 'I'm really sorry, but I have to go out in a while to give my brother a hand. I'll likely be away the best part of the day.'

Katie turned to the children, 'Looks like you'll need to come with me,' she said. 'I'm afraid we might have a bit of a wait on our hands.'

'I could take the children somewhere close by if there's somewhere they want to go,' offered Colin.

'What about the swimming pool?' suggested Katie.

'I'd like to go back to the museum at Kilmartin,' said

Emma. 'And when we are there we can get something to eat as well.'

'I'd be happy with that too,' said Ben. 'We were just at the pool the other day.'

'Well make sure you've got your phones with you and I'll phone or text you when I'm leaving the hospital.' Katie gave both children a hug. Then she jumped into the car, the engine roared into life, and they took off down the hill, pebbles spraying out in all directions.

An hour later Ben and Emma got out of Colin's car and waved him off as he swung the vehicle around to begin his return journey. Emma picked up the rucksack she had packed at the cottage and lifted it on to her shoulder before they moved into the grounds of the Kilmartin House Museum.

'It seems very quiet,' said Ben.

Emma shrugged her shoulders. 'That's because it's still early.'

But as they crossed the garden and neared the entrance they saw that the door was lying wide open. An unusually bright light could be seen inside and there was the sound of hammering and sawing. As they approached, a man in a grubby boiler suit stuck his head out of the doorway. 'Sorry kids, we're shut today.' The children stopped in their tracks. 'Did you not see the sign? We're changing the reception area today. We'll be open again tomorrow.'

Ben turned to face his sister. 'What are we going to do now?'

'Well, we could sit down for a start.' There was a garden bench a few feet from where they were standing. 'It looks like it's going to be a nice day,' mused Emma. 'We could take a walk across the fields and look at the cairns and stones again. And I think Temple Wood is nearby.' But then she seemed to have a change of mind and began rummaging in the rucksack. She pulled out a crumpled sweatshirt and a couple of apples and laid them down beside her, but they weren't what she was searching for.

'Here it is,' she said, pulling out the map she'd packed. 'Let's see what else there is to do around here.' The rucksack dropped to her feet. She unfolded the map and opened it out, spreading it across their legs. Once they got their bearings, the children examined the area around Kilmartin. Thanks to the activity of the last few days, they had recently visited much of it.

'There's Carnasserie Castle,' said Ben, pointing to the map. 'It looks quite close. I wonder what it's like?'

'We went there last time we were here. Remember Dad took us? That was where that big dog suddenly appeared and chased you down the path.' Emma shook with laughter at the memory. 'You got the fright of your life!'

'Very funny!' said Ben, and he gave her a shove. 'But wasn't it quite a good place to visit?'

'It was good enough,' admitted Emma. 'But it would be good to do something new.' There was silence for a while and then she spoke again. 'I've got an idea. Why don't we go up there?' Ben's gaze followed her finger. She had swivelled on the seat and was pointing up to the big hill behind the village.

'What's up there?'

'The hill is called Beinn Bhan. It's not that high. On the top of the hill is St Breccan's Cell. Colin told me about him. St Breccan was some kind of monk or holy man and that was where he went to be on his own. But Colin said that from there is the greatest view – not just a view of Kilmartin Glen but right across to Crinan and out to sea.'

Ben's brow furrowed and looked unsure. 'I've never climbed a hill like that before. And Mum won't be too pleased.'

But Emma was already trying to fold the map away. 'Come on, Ben. It's not *that* big a hill. I've climbed much bigger ones with Dad. And Mum is bound to be busy for a while. We've got our mobiles. And we've got to do *something*.' She got to her feet, refilling the rucksack. 'We don't have anything to eat in here. We can pick up some cans of juice and sandwiches at the store across the road.' As she walked away, Ben started tugging at the zip on his jacket. It was a warm day but he wondered if he would feel warm at the top of the hill.

The climb took much longer than Emma had expected. For one thing, there didn't seem to be any obvious pathway to follow. It didn't take them very long to wind their way through the trees that framed the village; soon they found that the terrain they were climbing on was open and exposed to the elements. But it seemed as if every time they managed to scramble to the top of a ridge, the ground in front of them would dip again and yet another ridge would stand up to torment them.

Instead of the rock climb that Emma was hoping for, the ground around them seemed to be boggy and wet. Ben was first to complain. 'This is like quicksand!'

'It's just a marsh. We'll be okay in a minute,' countered Emma, trying to sound confident.

'If I had known we were going to climb a hill I wouldn't

have worn these boots.'

Emma looked down at her brother's footwear. 'You've got nothing to complain about. I'm wearing trainers.'

At this, Ben stopped walking. 'This is crazy. We shouldn't be doing this. If Mum knew we were here, she'd – '

Emma cut him short. 'Well, she *doesn't* know. And she's busy. She'll text us before she comes to get us.'

A sudden movement in the bushes to their left caused both children to jump. Instinctively Emma reached out for Ben's arm. From out of the foliage moved a group of cows, heading slowly in their direction. Emma breathed a sigh of relief. 'Hey, it's just some cows.'

Ben frowned. 'How do you know they're cows? Maybe they're bulls.'

Emma tugged at her brother's sleeve. 'They aren't bulls. And they won't give us any trouble. Keep looking ahead, Ben. If you just look ahead, you'll see there isn't far to go.'

The children were breathless when they reached the top of the hill, but the scene that met their eyes more than made up for the tiredness of their limbs, and the few clouds overhead did little to limit the view.

Kilmartin lay spread out below them. For some reason, from this vantage point, the village seemed to have grown much bigger. They took in the wide expanse of valley spreading southwards from the church. It was easy to see a pattern to the various cairns and tombs scattered on the floor of the glen. Further still lay Crinan, its lighthouse, and the vast expanse of ocean beyond.

Emma was looking at the islands in the distance. She shouted over the wind to her brother. 'If you look over there, you will see Jura. And that's Islay,' she added for good measure. She spoke confidently but she wasn't sure she had got them in the right order. Then she turned her attention to the east. It was possible to make out a series of hills in the far distance. The peaks jutted up sharply, like the ones in a child's drawing. 'That's Arran over there,' she said. 'Glasgow's that direction too.'

'But what is *this*, right here?' Ben was pointing at the small pillar that stood beside them. It looked as if it was marking the topmost part of the hill.

Emma ran her hands along the concrete. 'It's called a trig point. I think it's used for measuring distances, but I'm not really sure.'

'What about the monk's cell?'

Emma's eyes now started following the line of the hill. 'We need to follow the top of this ridge. Colin said it's not far south of the trig point'.

The small path on the top of the hill fell away in front of them, sweeping downwards for about twenty feet before rising once again. Following it up with her eyes, Emma could see a large stone protruding from the heathery summit. 'Let's go. I think that's it over there. We can eat our lunch when we get there.' She started down the track, then turned to watch Ben follow. 'Watch your step. There's quite a drop here.'

As they sat together eating their lunch, even Emma had to admit that St Breccan's Cell was a bit of a disappointment. A few large jagged rocks pointed from the summit to the sky, but the rest of the site was no more than rubble. Grass grew where walls had once stood. 'Not very impressive,' she said. 'this place is so unbelievably small.'

Ben laughed out loud. 'This monk must have been the

size of a midge! I don't suppose he needed very much if he just wanted to be on his own. Maybe he lived most of the time somewhere else.'

Emma was propped up with her back against one of the bigger stones, her legs stretching into the cell. 'At least he had a great view, she said. 'I bet that's why he decided to come up here. This would be a great place for a lookout tower – you can see for miles.'

When Emma finally lifted herself up, she was holding a plastic bag. 'Stick your rubbish in that. Give me a minute or two. I'm going to go along here a bit and check if I can see a better route down this hill.' Placing the rucksack beside her brother, she left him to tidy up.

It was as Emma picked her way further along the path that a scream was heard – puncturing the silence of the hill. The high, piercing noise was wordless, but clearly human. Shaken and scared in equal measure, she swung around to look at her brother. The wind was blowing full into her face and as she steadied herself on the path, she had to push strands of hair away from her eyes. Then, as she looked at the ridge behind her, her body stiffened in shock.

A short distance ahead, the partially submerged stones of St Breccan's cell were clearly visible. Then there was nothing to be seen, but a vast expanse of empty sky. Ben had disappeared completely! Throwing herself forward, Emma started running back to the space where her brother had been. 'Ben!' she cried at the top of her voice, as she raced, leaping and sprinting along the ridge.

She came to a stop as she reached the ruin. She heard another noise as she pushed her way in between the rocks. Leaning over the side of the drop she could see Ben. But everything was wrong. His hands were stretched upwards, high above his head, and his legs were kicking wildly around him, desperately seeking a foothold.

As he lost his balance, Ben had frantically clawed in the air for support. His hands had fastened onto some heather growing where the large stones were sunk into the earth, and as he fell, his weight had ripped the plant and its roots out of the earth. Now the heather trailed downwards like twisted and gnarled ropes, and his body was swinging as he hung on desperately.

Quickly, Emma climbed down beside him, relieved to discover a small grassy ledge just below her brother's feet. She put her hand on his arm. His knuckles were white. 'You can let go of the heather,' she said. 'You won't fall from here.' Slowly, Ben released his grip. He looked at Emma's face which now was almost touching his own.

'I think I've twisted my ankle.' he said breathlessly. 'I don't know how I did it. It happened just as I was standing up.'

Emma looked down. There were only a couple of paces between her brother and a drop of hundreds of feet. She tried to reassure him. 'Don't worry. It could have been much worse. Give me your arm and we'll get back up to the ridge.' Emma felt both guilt and relief as she watched Ben sitting on a stone, nursing his ankle.

'I don't think I've broken anything. But my foot still feels sore.'

'Do you think you can walk?'

'I *think* so.' Then he paused for a moment. 'I *hope* so.'

'We'll need to take it easy going down this hill, but we better start moving right away.' Emma stole a glance at his phone. The reception seemed to be clearer up here than back at Achnabreck. *Must be to do with the altitude,* she told herself. She prayed that her mother wouldn't phone until they were safely down on ground level.

Meanwhile, Ben had crawled back to the scene of the drama and was cautiously peering over at the spot where he had fallen, and at the strange trail of undergrowth which he had managed to wrench from the side of the hill. 'You nearly pulled the whole mountain down with you,' joked Emma.

Then she saw the furrows appear on her brother's brow, before he spoke. 'What do you think *that* is?'

About twenty feet below them, they could see black earth, exposed to the sunlight now that the covering of heather had been ripped away. But there was something else newly visible – they could see a large slab of rock like the ones in the monk's cell. It seemed to have been evenly cut and it looked as if there were markings carved onto the surface of the stone.

Emma started to move downwards, her body positioned low towards the ground, but Ben called her back. 'Help me down beside you. I want to see it too.' She put her arm around her brother's shoulder and they descended the slope together.

It only took a few minutes to pull away some of the remaining heather and clear the soil. Soon they were looking at a roughly rectangular piece of rock. The carving was at the very centre of the stone. There were no strange prehistoric symbols, spirals or crosses. Instead the inscription contained three words – unknown but unmistakable.

'FIACHRA AGUS MOR'.

The children looked at each other.

'What do you think it means?' asked Ben.

'I've got no idea,' said Emma. 'But it has to mean something.'

THE RETURN

Gris, son of Ketil, stopped examining his sword and stuck it back into his belt. Then he leaned over, spitting into the water. It was time to pay careful attention, now that he was posted to the front of the ship. The galley was making good progress up the loch, for although there was little wind; the men had taken to the oars and were pulling hard against the current.

The day was dull but not at all cold. Nonetheless Gris felt himself shiver – it was the sense of anticipation he always felt before a battle, and it was more excitement than fear. He knew that the men, who sat together behind him on either side of the ship straining at the oars, would be feeling just the same. Each one was a battle-hardened warrior of many campaigns; fighting was in their blood.

The longship cut through the water as it passed the wide opening of Loch Gilp. Today their destination lay a few miles further north. As the water narrowed, Gris could see the hills of Glendaruel on the opposite bank, but they continued to stick closely to the western coast. The giant man undid the clasp on his cloak and let the heavy material fall from his shoulders. He would leave it behind him when they landed.

'Father,' Gris barked down the length of the galley. 'You should come here now.' From the makeshift cabin at the stern of the ship Ketil now appeared. As he moved forward to the bow, he paused to look up at the mast. The square mainsail above him was as black as night. On the deck immediately underneath sat two men with chains on their legs, their hair cut short as was the Viking custom with slaves. Only minutes before, their task had been to move among the adventurers around them, passing out strong beer; heavy drinking always preceded an attack. Along the length of the ship were rows of shields fastened to the gunwales by brackets on the sides of the boat. Each shield had its own design. In less favourable weather, they would act as a protection against the wind and spray, but today his men would pull them free as they prepared for combat

Ketil came to stand beside his son. His clothing was dark, though the distinctive helmet on his head gleamed silver when the sunlight pierced through the clouds. Ketil's beard was darker than Gris's golden mane, with few flecks of grey despite his advancing years. He was a tall, powerfully-built man, but even he seemed small beside the younger man. 'We are nearly there,' said Gris.

Ketil's eyes scanned the loch in all directions, and then he began to nod his head. A smile formed on his lips. 'It is good to be back.' Now it was his turn to look to the back of the boat. 'Bring the boy,' he commanded. Runolf moved forward, dragging a length of rope. On the other end of the rope was a young man with his hands bound in front. As he reached the standing figures, Runolf's leg shot out and the young man crashed painfully to the deck. The youth's hair was roughly pulled back, forcing his head up so he had to meet the gaze of his master.

Ketil continued to smile as he looked at the boy who had been forced to kneel at his feet. He looked about seventeen, still too young for a beard. He was a good-looking young man though his face was disfigured by an ugly scar that cut into his forehead above his left eye. 'What is it like to be home again, Fiachra?'

As he looked out towards the shoreline, Fiachra knew exactly where he was. In a few minutes they would arrive at the opening of the bay. He had never approached Asknish by boat before but the views of the loch around him were unmistakable. Of course Asknish was never his home but *that* lay only a few miles north-west from here. And Alba was his homeland.

Fiachra's last memory of this place was now three years old, when a club had smashed into his head, knocking him senseless. He could only remember the searing pain, the sudden darkness, his legs buckling from under him … and nothing more. What happened next that day was lost to him.

★ ★ ★

The two Norsemen had descended the hill carrying Fiachra, and had moved across to the shingle of the beach. Smoke swirled around everyone on the shore as the houses of the village were swallowed by flames. There was the smell of burning wood and the sound of pigs being butchered. Without ceremony, the body of

Fiachra was dropped at the feet of Ketil. As he paused to regain his breath, one of the soldiers pointed to the hill behind him. 'We gave chase only for this … a boy.'

'Why didn't you kill him?'

'That we can easily do. But we thought you might like to see him first and decide his fate. He looks like nothing but he fought like a wildcat. He killed Guthrum.' The man raised his arm. There was a wooden club in his hand. 'I hit him with this.'

Ketil raised an eyebrow as he looked down at the crumpled figure at his feet. 'This? This child? This bag of bones killed Guthrum?'

'Let's finish him now!' demanded Gris, as his hand moved instinctively to his sword hilt.

A loud snarl was heard. 'We could kill him more slowly.' Runolf, who loved to torture his opponents, had moved forward to join his father and brother. His long black hair was pasted to his face with blood. Still hungry for more killing, his eyes gleamed wildly, as he gazed down at the boy.

'We'll keep him for now. Take the wildcat onto the ship,' demanded Ketil. 'If he lives we may find some use for him.' It was clear the older man had some idea in his head, unknown to his sons, but he could sense their disappointment. As he turned away he patted Runolf's shoulder; 'Don't worry. We can kill him anytime.'

*   *   *

Three years had now passed – three long years of living in Norway – three long, hard years of being a slave to Ketil the Cruel. During that time Fiachra had learned the basics of the Norse language. He began by noting the curses that were directed at him and the other slaves around him at the

Viking camp. But in time, he began to pick up the general conversation, and it was clear that this was a skill that Ketil wished him to acquire. He came to understand that he might prove useful to them in future raids – being able to speak Gaelic, unlike any of the Norsemen in Ketil's company. Yet over the next two years he remained where he was while the raiding party set out for weeks at a time. He was never told where they had been, but from what little he overheard, it was likely to have been somewhere on Alba's west coast.

The Viking camp and adjoining farm were set on the shores of a narrow loch which the locals called a fjord. All around them, the giant hills swept majestically downwards from the clouds before plunging steeply into the water. It was beautiful, though bleak in the winter months. Despite the extreme cold, it reminded Fiachra of his home. As long as the slaves did exactly as they were told, the Vikings were not too harsh with them. The slaves were needed to work on the farm, and if they kept fit and well, some of them could make money for their captors when they were sold on.

Fiachra guessed that he was being kept on at the farm for some purpose. Though the two sons loved to abuse him, sometimes Riupa, Ketil's wife, spoke some kind words to him or sneaked him some extra food, especially when her husband was away travelling or hunting in the hills.

Fiachra learned the skill of patience for he knew that he could do nothing but bide his time. Escape from his captors was out of the question. But he wanted more than just to be free of them. He longed to be back in his own land, and he knew he would never get there on his own.

Thanks to Gris and Runolf, he had also learned to fight. They used him as a sparring partner when they were bored –

and that was often. All Viking warriors loved fighting, and when there were no enemies to confront they looked to each other for entertainment. Fiachra was not as skilled or as strong as either of them and he often ended up much the worse for wear. But that was happening less often now; he was always quicker than the brothers and his skills were developing. He knew he had greatly improved on the basic training that his father Cuan had offered him in happier times. He now felt proficient with sword and bow, though as yet, he had rarely even handled an axe, the favoured weapon of his captors.

He discovered that Magnus Barefoot had become King of Norway only after a long struggle with a rival king, called Haakon. Once he was king in his own right, Magnus had set about extending the Norse kingdom in Alba and Ireland, as many of his countrymen wanted to settle in these new territories. However, Ketil, as an old ally of Haakon, preferred to conduct his own raiding trips. He was more interested in murder, looting and scavenging than in living peacefully in a new land. To many of his fellow Norsemen, Ketil the Cruel was no more than a pirate.

*   *   *

Now Ketil's steely fingers dug deep into Fiachra's shoulder as he pulled him roughly to his feet at the bow of the ship. 'This is your time to repay us for looking after you, Fiachra. Do as I say today and you will be rewarded. But you have to earn our trust. If you betray us, then …' Ketil's eyes shot across to Runolf, as a warning to the Scot. Gris smiled. He knew how much his brother would love to organise a long, slow death for Fiachra.

Fiachra found his voice. 'What do you want me to do?'

'We need information – which you can get for us. After you've had a chance to see your old village again.'

The village of Asknish regularly filled Fiachra's thoughts. He remembered that Breccan had left the village before the attack and he hoped the priest was still alive. He wondered if anyone had returned to rebuild the village. Most of all he dreamed of Mor, and prayed that somehow she had escaped. If he could find a way to get free from his captors, he would search for as long as it took to find her.

A sharp sound came across the wind to the longship from further up the coast. For the invaders, the sound was not welcome. It was the pealing of a bell. Someone in Asknish was sounding an alarm. 'I said we should have come at night,' said Runolf.

His father laughed. 'Do not worry, my son. They won't get far before we cut them down.' Almost as he spoke, the small bay of Loch Gair came into view and the first thing they saw looked to be the home of the bell. Ahead of them, on the far shore, stood a chapel. It was on the same site as the previous church, but though it remained small in size, it was built solidly of stone.

As they rounded the point, the village itself became visible. As Fiachra looked, it appeared to be much the same as before and he marvelled that a place could reinvent itself in such a short time. The wooden houses by the shore looked familiar, but this time there was a strange silence. There was no band of defenders waiting for them.

By the time the boat beached itself on the shingle, most of the Vikings had already flung themselves into the surf and were making for the trees on either side of the bay. Each one of them carried an axe and a round shield. 'We just need one alive,' barked Ketil at the departing backs of his men. It took only a few minutes before some raiders returned, dragging an old man with them across the stones of the beach. As they threw him roughly onto the sand at the feet of their leader, Ketil turned to Fiachra and spoke quietly. 'Find out where the people are.'

'What will happen to him? You must spare his life.'

'If he gives us the information, then he will live.'

Fiachra dropped to his knees beside the captured man. For a moment he wondered if the man was breathing. He tried to move the old man's head, but it was difficult with his own hands still bound together in front of him. When the man at last opened his eyes, Fiachra began to speak.

'Listen to me. I am Fiachra of Ederline.' There was a gasp of surprise from the man on the ground, although Fiachra didn't recognise him. 'I am the son of Cuan.' The man was slowly nodding; he began to breathe heavily. 'You must tell me where everyone has gone.' said Fiachra. 'If you tell me, you will live.'

The man looked doubtful, and did not open his mouth. It was time to take a risk. Fiachra leaned closer to the man. 'Listen. They don't know what I'm saying. They don't understand. Tell me where the people of Asknish have gone, and I will send the Vikings another way. I want to save lives – including yours.'

Now the man pulled himself up on his elbow. 'Birdfield. They've gone to Birdfield.' Fiachra knew that place was a few miles to the north. But the man seemed confused. 'Tell them that. Tell them Birdfield.'

'Where *have* they gone?'

'They've gone to the crannogs at Loch Glashan.'

'I need to know something else. Do you know a girl called Mor? She used to live here. And there was a priest called Breccan.'

The old man returned his gaze. 'They are both with the others.' Joy and hope surged through Fiachra, and he had to stop himself from crying out – Mor and Breccan both alive, and so close to him!

A rough hand pulled him upwards.

'What did he say?'

'He said they have gone north to Birdfield.'

'Birdfield?'

'It's only a few miles from here.'

Ketil swung his cloak over his shoulder and started walking off the beach. 'Gather everyone together,' he instructed. And to Gris, 'Bring the boy.' There was a muffled, choking scream from the man on the ground. With a smile on his face, Runolf slowly climbed to his feet, blood dripping from a long knife. Fiachra shouted at the disappearing figure of Ketil. 'You promised to spare his life.'

But the Viking leader continued walking towards the trees without once looking back.

ALONG THE SHORE

Two of the Norsemen soon returned from scouting the path, and confirmed that there were footprints and tracks leading north along the shore towards the next settlement. Fiachra breathed a sigh of relief. He was glad that the path was so regularly used by travellers.

After a few minutes of preparation they set off north along the coast road, leaving four disappointed raiders to wait with the longship. There was no need for the Vikings to hurry. Better let the frightened natives reach Birdfield before attacking them. That way they could kill everyone at once, ransack another village, and return to Asknish to burn it once more.

Ketil wondered if there might be some rich takings from the church, which looked much more substantial than on his last visit. He had no interest in holy books but there might be gold or silver in candlesticks, crosses or plates, and perhaps coins given to the chapel by the faithful. Ketil despised the Christian faith and its message of peace and love. This new religion had spread to his own country and been embraced by many. But he had always served the old gods, and it suited him to keep to the old ways.

As they marched along the pathway, Fiachra's head was spinning with thoughts and emotions. For three years he had waited for this opportunity to be back in his own land. He had prayed that Mor and Breccan might still be alive. Now he felt he could almost hear the sound of his heart beating with joy at the news he had just been given. But his heart was also racing hard with terror and anxiety at the dilemma he faced.

On the one hand, he would have only one chance to make his escape. If he failed, he would die. On the other hand, if he did not make his move quickly, he was helping to lead this band of savages to a new group of innocent victims. Fiachra cast his mind back to the last time he had passed through Birdfield. It had always been a very small hamlet, even compared to the village of Asknish. Fiachra could not live with the thought that he had helped to lead a group of killers to attack his neighbours.

The path led them uphill and away from the side of the loch. For a time, the water was hidden from view. Now the road was descending again and glimpses of water could be seen through the trees. But all the time Fiachra was looking the other way, up to the trees and the hills on his left.

Ketil turned to look at the young man who had drawn level with him. 'Lord Ketil,' began Fiachra, 'we will soon arrive at Birdfield. But there is a place over there where you can see the village plainly.' Ketil looked up to the craggy rocks that were now on view on a nearby hill. 'Up there is a ledge that I have climbed often. There you can see Loch Fyne clearly in all directions. And you can also see the houses at Birdfield.'

The Viking looked at him with suspicion. 'Why are you telling me this?'

Fiachra swallowed hard. 'I have lived with you for three years now. You still have to decide whether you are ready to trust me. I want to be useful to you because I want to live. I know that you have never seen the village ahead, so from that ledge you can plan your attack.'

For a moment Ketil seemed interested. Then he snorted. 'I've not got time for this.'

Fiachra tried not to sound desperate. 'It would only take a few minutes.'

Ketil raised his arm to halt the marchers and called for Egill, a quick-footed young man who had earlier been sent ahead to check the trail. Like his leader, he was still wearing his cloak. 'The boy tells me that up there is a ledge where you can spy on the village.' Egill concentrated his gaze on the wall of rock that rose up beyond the trees, but he couldn't make out a ledge.

'I can take him up and point out the way,' offered Fiachra. The older man nodded an agreement. Then Fiachra lifted his hands out in front of him. 'Please release my hands.'

Ketil looked at him blankly. 'Why would I do that?'

'Because we have to climb these rocks. I need to be able to move freely.'

Without changing his expression Ketil produced a knife and sliced through the ropes in one movement. But then he called over for another of his men. 'Ubbe, you go with them both. Keep your eye on Fiachra.' Ubbe was a tall thick-set man with enormous arms. The shield he carried on his back looked to Fiachra to be the size of a door. Apart from Gris, he was the largest Norseman in this raiding party. Fiachra's heart sank.

Ketil's company waited by the shoreline while the three men moved away from the water and started slowly climbing the hill. The slope was gentle at first and thick with trees. Soon they could not be seen. Then the incline increased and they had to use their hands to pull themselves upwards on the stones. By the time they emerged above the trees, there was only rock under their feet. All the time Egill was climbing within touching distance of Fiachra, and the large shape of Ubbe followed behind.

Fiachra looked carefully at the man by his side. Despite the climb, Egill was still wearing his cloak and it billowed and swung around him with every step. As Fiachra considered his plan he realised that the cloak could be a complication. Underneath, tucked into the belt of Egill's tunic, was a small dagger. It would be Fiachra's only chance.

They continued on, his heart pounding faster and faster. There was sweat on his body, but only partly due to the exertions of the climb. Fear was gripping him with every movement. He prayed that his memory of this place was serving him well.

Suddenly the cliff came into view. To reach their destination, they just had to scramble over some boulders. The task was not difficult as the rocks were set into the side of the hill, but the route was narrow and on one side was only empty air, with a steep drop to the ground far below them. Fiachra's arm was shaking as he pointed straight ahead. 'There is the ledge,' said Fiachra, breathing heavily.

'I'll go first,' said Egill, 'and then you come after me.' Fiachra nodded. It was what he had expected to hear. The Norseman bent forwards and started hauling himself over the narrow rocks. As he crawled onto the ledge, and started to climb to his feet, Fiachra was close at his back.

Everything happened at once. Crouching down low, Fiachra suddenly stretched forward, pulling the dagger out and away from Egill's belt. In the same movement, Fiachra wheeled around to face the man behind him. Ubbe's hands were planted on the final boulder, steadying himself before finding his balance on the ledge. Fiachra's boot thudded into his side with force, taking him completely by surprise. Then the tall warrior was gone, hurtling silently to the forest floor beneath.

As Egill swung round to face Fiachra, the younger man hurled himself towards him and their bodies crashed together. Both of them collapsed to the ground, Fiachra's hand reaching out for Egill's throat in an attempt to prevent him from shouting out. But the Norseman's strength was superior, and a solid punch from his fist sent Fiachra sprawling onto the rock shelf. He felt dizzy and winded by the blow.

As Egill reached behind him to release the axe he had been wearing on his back, Fiachra realised he had no time to wait for his head to clear. Pitching himself forward at the Viking in front of him he plunged his blade under the ribs of his opponent. Egill fell backwards against the rock, and slowly toppled to the ground. He lay still and lifeless as Fiachra pulled himself to his feet. He put the knife into his own belt, moved to the drop and looked over the edge to where Ubbe had fallen. There was no sound, and nothing to see in the shadows below.

Fiachra scrambled down the rock face and set out northwards. He desperately wanted to go south straight away and get to Loch Glashan, but he knew he must leave a trail to keep the Vikings heading in the wrong direction. So he plunged into the darkness of the wood around him, moving as fast as he was able, weaving past trees and vaulting streams. As he ran, he realised that his life was now in mortal danger. But he knew also that, for the first time in three years, he was free.

ON THE ISLAND

It was getting dark when Fiachra nearly stumbled into the water at the northern end of Loch Glashan. He began picking his way along the shoreline, exhausted and breathless, exhilarated to be free, but mostly excited to imagine that he was drawing near to Mor.

Thick trees covered the hills and surrounded the loch on all sides. There were oak, beech and ash, and wherever they began to thin, there was bushes and dense bracken to push though. The journey took longer than he had hoped. For most of the way there was only silence, occasionally broken by the sound of a gull overhead – a reminder that the sea was not far away, though not visible from the hills around Loch Glashan.

Fiachra had never approached the settlement from this direction before, as the shortest route was to climb the path from Asknish on the coast. He was beginning to wonder if his sense of direction had failed him when he noticed the shape of the islands rising in the gathering gloom ahead of him.

There were two settlements on the water. One was built on a natural island, and Fiachra could see five or six buildings there of various sizes. This was where most of the people lived. Close by was the crannog, a man-made island of wood, supported by wooden stilts and posts driven deep into the bed of the loch. Most of the craftsmen had their workshops here and this was where Fiachra had been before with his father Cuan.

The craftsmen at Glashan were much in demand, supplying the fortress and market of Dunadd with fine goods of metal and leather. There were stone carvers here too, their work well known across the country. Over the years their services had found favour with bishops and kings.

As he drew near to the settlements, he could see that the boats for the crannog were moored on the island, and that a stone causeway connected the island to the shore. Shafts of light were visible in some of the buildings, but otherwise there were no sign of life. Just as Fiachra thought he might reach the island without seeing a living soul, a shout was heard from the undergrowth to his left.

'Come no further!' From under the shadow of the trees stepped a short man, brandishing a spear. As he spoke, he prodded Fiachra with the point of the weapon. 'What do you want here?' demanded the stranger.

'I have come here looking for you. I am Fiachra from Ederline.'

The stranger looked from head to toe at the new visitor. 'Ederline? I don't think so! No one from Ederline dresses like that. You are a Norseman.' Fiachra looked down at the boots he was wearing. They were much more substantial than any shoes he had owned before. He realised that all the clothes on his back had come from his captors.

'Have you ever heard a Norseman talk like this?' he said. 'I am Fiachra from Ederline and Cuan was my father. He was killed when Ketil the Cruel attacked Asknish and I have been his prisoner for these past three years.'

'And now you come here, leading the Vikings to us.' The sentry continued to regard him with suspicion.

'I pray I have not done that,' replied Fiachra. 'The Vikings landed again at Asknish today but I led them away north along the coast. I did what I could but I fear they may be on my trail. I have come here to warn you.'

The sentry gestured with his arm towards the island. 'Then you will have an audience with Conaing.'

Fiachra continued walking, with the spearman at his back. When they got to the stone causeway Fiachra could see there was a substantial gap in the walkway. A long length of wood, made up of three planks bound together, served as a portable bridge. It lay on the banks of the island.

As they drew near, the sentry shouted out a greeting, and two men emerged from the darkness and started bridging the gap with the planks. Fiachra began to cross the bridge, with the sentry at his heels. A wooden fence surrounded the whole settlement, and as the two walked through the open gateway, they arrived at an expanse of open ground. The various turf-roofed buildings were arranged haphazardly around the circle of grass.

From the doorway of the biggest dwelling, a man emerged and started moving towards Fiachra. He wore a stone-coloured tunic and a sword was belted at his side. A

71

dark brown cloak hung from his shoulders, held in place with a silver brooch. The man was staring at Fiachra, but when he spoke it was to the spearman behind him.

'Who is this?'

Fiachra replied for himself. 'I am Fiachra, son of Cuan of Ederline.'

The man peered at Fiachra in the darkness. 'We thought you had been killed with your father when Asknish was raided.'

'I was taken prisoner by Ketil. I have only managed to escape today.'

'My name is Conaing. I am the leader here. Your father was a good man. Come inside and we will hear your story.'

As Fiachra bent down and stepped through the low doorway, he was amazed to see so many people crammed inside. The warmth, the smell of cooking, and the promise of a sheltered place to sleep were all inviting prospects but as he looked around him, he realised that there was only one person he really wanted to see.

A low fire burned in the middle of the floor, which was surrounded by packed earth; people lined the sides of the room, sitting, lying and standing. Fiachra was led over to the fire and told to sit down beside Conaing. As he squatted down on the dirt floor his eyes continued their gaze. The billowing smoke and the dark corners of the building made it impossible to see everyone, but there was certainly no sign of Mor or Breccan.

Everyone sat silently, staring at him and his strange clothes, until he finished relating his story. Then Conaing explained what had happened after the people of Asknish had climbed up to the loch. 'We saw the ship, and we realised we are all in great danger. But some people here are too old to run any further. Until help arrives, we have decided to make our stand on this island. We have some weapons and the island will give us some defence. There is food enough here to last a week.'

Fiachra could wait no longer to ask his question. 'I heard that Mor is here.' Then he added, 'And the priest, Breccan.' As he spoke, he was hoping that they might suddenly step forward, out from the darkness. But nobody moved.

'Mor and Breccan are not here,' said Conaing. 'They have set off to get help. We gave them our two best horses. Mor is young and fit but she is no warrior. And Breccan will not fight. It was agreed that they should go on behalf of us all to speak to the chief at Dunadd. The coast road is too dangerous. They had to go west over the hills. But Breccan knows the glens around us. He often has to visit the churches at Kilmichael and Kilbride.'

Fiachra was disappointed, but also relieved that his friends would at least be safer on the road to the fort at Dunadd than waiting on this island. 'Is Lochlann still the chief?'

Conaing nodded. 'You are right. He is not known as a man of action, but he holds his land on behalf of King Edgar and he is duty-bound to maintain the peace. If the Vikings are successful here, they may decide to burrow deeper into Lochlann's territory. They might even be bold enough to attack Dunadd itself. So we trust he will come to us with aid.' As Fiachra looked at Conaing through the smoke, he could see a smile beginning to form on his face. 'You look tired, Fiachra. And it's no wonder. Tonight you must get what rest you can.'

It was great to be able to drink some milk and beer and enjoy the taste of fresh meat and vegetables. On the voyage from Norway there had been only dried meat and water. To sleep indoors on a straw mattress also seemed like a luxury compared to the leather sacks they used along the deck of the longship. Fiachra was shown to a space. As he lay down he looked at the people nearest to him. They seemed to be either very young or very old. There was no one that he recognised. Despite his tiredness, Fiachra didn't sleep quickly. His head was swimming with worries and thoughts.

When he woke the next morning and stepped outside to examine his surroundings, the sky was black and overcast. Around the island, the water was choppy and the wind much stronger. The bridge was in place, joining the causeway to the shore and people were crossing in either direction. A few men were acting as sentries, keeping watch over the paths that led towards the island. A circular fence of timber protected the inhabitants; this barricade – the height of a grown man – included most of the island.

The livestock – cows, pigs, chickens and a couple of horses – were in the open air, having been displaced by the arrival of refugees from the village below them on the coast. Fiachra reckoned there must be at least fifty people altogether. They outnumbered the Vikings, but there were many women among the group of Gaels and some of the men were too old or too young to fight.

A woman offered Fiachra a bowl of porridge, and he sat overlooking the water while he ate. After a few minutes he felt someone sitting down beside him. 'My name is Cathal.' Fiachra turned to the man on his left. He was middle aged with a short beard and dark red hair which hung down in pleats over his shoulders. Like most of the other men he wore a coarse stone-coloured tunic above his leggings, but over the tunic he had a sleeveless leather waistcoat.

'I'm one of the leather workers here. I live on the island, though some of the other workers have their workshops over there.' He was pointing across to the crannog. 'Anyway, I knew your father Cuan. He was a good man. And he was a good craftsman. In a way we were rivals because we made many of the same things. But I always thought he was envious of us.'

'Why did you think that?'

'Well, we are able to work from here and we only need to transport our goods to Dunadd. We have regular customers and we make a living. It seems as if your father had to travel up and down the length and breadth of the country to seek buyers.'

'That was his way,' said Fiachra. 'My father liked to travel. He preferred being on the road, especially after my mother died.'

The two seated men looked up as Conaing strode over towards them. 'Cathal, Fergus is checking over the weapons we have. Could you give him a hand?' As the leather worker got to his feet, Conaing looked down at the young man on the ground, finishing off the remains of his porridge. 'Did you sleep well, Fiachra?'

'I did, and now I would be happy to make myself useful.'

'Could you take a turn at watching the path down to Asknish?' Fiachra stood up. 'Speak to Fergus or Cathal and ask them for a spear,' said Conaing.

As Fiachra moved between the houses on the island, he realised that most of the women and children remained inside the buildings. But one woman moved towards him and took hold of his arm. A long scarf almost entirely covered her dark hair. 'My name is Etain.'

Fiachra looked blank. She smiled at him. 'I am Mor's Aunt. Orlaith was my sister.' Now it was Fiachra's turn to grab her arm.

'I am so pleased to meet you,' he said. 'Can you tell me about Mor?'

'She will be so happy to know that you are alive, Fiachra. She says you saved her life. But no one ever knew what had become of you, because you were never found. Everyone else was killed that day. It was believed that you must have been killed too.'

'Everyone *was* killed,' agreed Fiachra, 'But I see that there are people again living in Asknish.'

'When Breccan came back and discovered what had happened, he took control. He gave a Christian burial to those who had been murdered. He invited people to come to Asknish and help rebuild the village. He was determined that the chapel should be properly finished and that the community should live again. Some new people came and helped him. But now as you can see they have had to come up here to us and Asknish is empty again.'

'Maybe not for long, Etain. If we can drive these Vikings away there may yet be peace for Asknish.'

'We need the soldiers to come from Dunadd if that is to happen. We will never defeat these Norsemen on our own.'

'How is Mor?' Fiachra asked again.

'She is well, Fiachra. She has remained good friends with Breccan and they often talk together. After the tragedy she came up the hill to Loch Glashan and has been living with me on the crannog. She has been a good help to me and my husband Dallin, though he has been saying lately it is time she started looking for a husband. She is seventeen years old now.'

'I know that well,' said Fiachra. 'I can't wait to see her again.'

They parted, Etain ducking low to enter a darkened building. Fiachra looked up to the ever-blackening clouds above. Rain was not far away. As he walked, he became aware of a shadow moving along the ground. A burly man was heading towards him. He was walking unevenly and it appeared as if he was trying to speak, but though his mouth opened and closed, no sound could be heard. Then a small trickle of blood began to ooze from his lips. Suddenly the man pitched forwards onto the grass. The shaft of an arrow protruded from his back.

Before Fiachra could begin to speak, the sound of Conaing's voice was heard booming out. 'Attack! We're under attack! Get everyone onto the island and draw the bridge across!'

Three people could be seen rushing over the causeway bridge before it was roughly pulled back onto the safety of the island. A fourth man could be seen running out from the trees, but suddenly he lost his footing, landing heavily on the grass. He didn't move. Fiachra was too far away to make out what had happened to him, but it seemed likely he too had been hit by a bowman. Another arrow thudded into a wooden post, inches from Fiachra's head, as he followed the direction that he had seen Cathal take. From behind the furthest building Cathal, and Fergus a stonemason, were handing out weapons to those around them.

'Here, Fiachra,' said Cathal, as he flung a spear towards the boy. Fiachra caught it in one hand but he was looking at the other weapons. He set the spear down on the ground and picked up a long bow. Clutching some arrows, he ran over to the cover afforded by the barricade. He began scanning the trees by the shore, looking for the Norsemen. A loud shout was heard as the Vikings appeared by the shore. It was their familiar war cry, well known to Fiachra. And finally, out of the darkness afforded by the trees, strode Ketil himself.

Fiachra could feel the adrenaline surging through his system. His heart was beating rapidly and his breathing raced. He tried not to think about what might happen to him if he were to fall into the hands of the Norsemen after he had betrayed them. But he knew that the short stretch of water between the defenders and the shore made them safe for now.

All the women and children were now inside the buildings, and most of the men who were able to fight were pressed along the perimeter of the fence. They were holding swords, spears or axes – none of which were of any use against the Norsemen on the shore However, at that distance, apart from the four Viking warriors who had bows, the invaders were equally unable to inflict any damage on the villagers.

In the centre of the island stood Conaing with Fergus at his side. The leader barked out instructions to the men around the fence. In various places stood collections of buckets of all sizes, brimming with water. Some of the men were emptying the contents over the turf roofs of the buildings and onto the wood of the fence itself. The biggest danger they faced was from flaming arrows. If the village was set alight, they would have no escape.

But the action seemed to be over as quickly as it had begun. There seemed to be a stalemate. Fiachra could see Ketil pacing backwards and forwards in front of his men. His arms were gesturing wildly as he spoke – something he tended to do when he was angry; but his words were out of earshot.

In the settlement, Conaing stood up, having examined the body of the large man who had collapsed in front of Fiachra. 'He is dead.'

'So is Broccan,' said another man. 'He was killed before he could reach the bridge.'

Conaing looked around him. 'Is there anyone else not accounted for?'

'What about Baetan?' said Fergus. 'He was keeping watch on the path to Asknish.'

A murmur went round the assembled men. No one had seen him. Fiachra felt himself shiver. This was the man he had been about to replace.

The Vikings looked down at the water in front of them and pondered their next move. Conaing called his men together. 'You come too, Fiachra,' he said. 'You know who we are dealing with.' They stood talking in the shadow of the first building. 'We just need to hold our nerve till help arrives,' said Conaing. 'As long as they don't smoke us out they can't get us easily. We just need to stay under cover to avoid their arrows.'

Cathal looked over towards Fiachra. 'How strong are they?'

'There are about forty men,' he replied.

'And they are bloodthirsty killers,' added Conaing. 'We have no chance of defeating them in open battle. We must wait right here.'

Another man spoke up in a frail voice. His hair was thick, but white. He looked like the oldest of the group.

'How do we know help is coming?'

Cathal replied. 'We don't know. But we must pray that it is coming – and coming soon. It's our only hope.'

THE END
OF THE WORLD

The tense silence lasted for over an hour. During that time, the rain relentlessly drove at the watchers by the fence, soaking their clothes and distorting their visibility. The sky was so dark that by mid-afternoon, it was as if night was falling.

Fiachra saw some movement in the trees by the shore. As some of the Norsemen made their way forward to the water, he kept his attention on Ketil and his distinctive silver helmet. But it was not Ketil who spoke. It was one of the villagers, Baetan, from the Glashan island. Standing behind him was Runolf, pressing a long dagger against his throat. The terror in his voice was obvious as Baetan started calling out towards the island, 'Conaing! Conaing!'

Conaing now climbed onto the fence. 'I can hear you.'

'I have a message from Ketil. He gives you one hour to

leave this place. If you leave, no harm will come to you – or to any of us. He wants to see what goods are kept on the island and he wants to take some livestock. But if you go now, no one will be harmed – except for one.'

'What do you mean?' asked Conaing.

'You must hand over Fiachra to Ketil. Everyone else can go free.'

Conaing shouted across the water, 'Who is this Fiachra?'

There followed some muffled voices before Baetan replied, 'Ketil knows that Fiachra is with you. He has been following his trail.'

The white haired man walked up to Conaing and shook his shoulder. 'We should do as they say. That way we will live.'

'But Fiachra will die,' said Conaing. The old man looked over to Fiachra. 'Forgive me, but it is better that one die than all of us perish.'

Cathal shot back at him. 'Are you mad? They cannot be trusted. If we try to leave they will kill us all.'

Conaing agreed. 'Cathal is right. Only on this island are we safe.'

There was one more shout from the banks of the loch. 'You have one hour to leave.' Then Runolf dragged Baetan back into the trees and the Vikings disappeared from view.

Conaing strode over to where Fiachra stood and grasped his shoulder. 'Don't worry,' he said quietly, 'We will stick together.' As Conaing gave this reassurance, one of the islanders drew back his bow and released an arrow after the departing Norsemen. It crashed through the trees and headed into the darkness beyond.

'Hold your fire!' This time Conaing's voice was for all to

hear. 'Do not waste arrows. We have few enough of them, and at this time they are our only defence.'

The men of the island gathered in a circle once more as they discussed Ketil's offer. Everyone was given a chance to say their piece. Most agreed with Cathal and Conaing, that the Norsemen would be unlikely to keep to their word, and would probably kill them all as they tried to leave the island. Nonetheless, Fiachra had the uncomfortable feeling that some of the men were staring at him as if somehow he was the one responsible for the Viking attack.

The conversation turned to anticipating the Vikings' next move. It seemed as if they had two options: to try to set fire to the village and force everyone out; or to attempt to cross over to the island themselves, either by building their own bridge or by using rafts.

'Either way, they are probably just biding their time for now,' said Fergus. 'They've given us an hour to make a response.'

'Refill the water buckets, and let's try to eat something,' said Conaing. 'Who knows when we will next be able to eat again together.'

Fiachra joined some of the other men at the furthest side of the island where the water of the loch flowed underneath the fence, and they started refilling the water buckets. He wondered whether this action was really needed as heavy rain continued to pour down on the people, animals and buildings within the enclosure. Although his stomach was rumbling, he didn't eat anything.

'I don't understand how Baetan is able to speak with the Vikings,' Fiachra said to Fergus. 'None of the men in Ketil's company can speak our language.'

'But Baetan can speak Norse,' replied Fergus.

'How so?'

'Baetan travels often in Cin Tire and trades with the Norsemen who have settled there. Not all the Vikings behave like savages. Many of them are living here peacefully. Even Cathal knows a bit of Norse.'

Fiachra was surprised at this news. It seemed that much had happened since he had been away.

Back at his station by the fence, Fiachra examined the bow that he had collected. It was nearly as long as Fiachra was tall, and it seemed to be well made. Beside him were eight arrows; he picked up one of them as he drew back the bow to get a feel for the weapon. He knew he was a good shot, but eight arrows wouldn't last very long.

Then came a shout from the man guarding the gate. Baetan and the Vikings had returned to the shoreline. Conaing and Cathal climbed onto the fence near the entrance to the enclosure. Fiachra kept watch from further along the rampart. Baetan shouted over towards them, Runolf still beside him brandishing his knife. 'Ketil is sorry that you did not take your chance to leave.'

Conaing shouted back, 'We do not think we can trust Ketil. But tell him we will offer him a deal. If he releases you to us unharmed, we will give him animals, and wine for his journey home.'

A few minutes passed while Baetan passed the message on to his captors. Then Ketil could be heard laughing loudly. Fiachra heard another voice cry out. It was Runolf. 'This is what we think of your plan, and this is what we will do to you!' His arm swung backwards and forwards swiftly, and Baetan dropped to his knees, blood spurting from his neck. Then his body collapsed onto the ground by the shore.

A cry of horror went up from those on the island who had witnessed the event. But Fiachra was moving too. Steadying himself against the fence, he had raised his bow and gathered an arrow from the ground beside him. Runolf stood arrogantly with legs apart, smiling towards them with the bloody knife held aloft in his hand. Fiachra knew he only had a few seconds to make his shot.

He took a deep breath, trying to relax his grip on the bow. He knew that in such an extreme situation, he might hold the weapon too tightly and his shot would veer off to one side. As Fiachra pulled the bow to its full draw, he half-closed his eyes. Even at this distance he fancied he could see the madness shining in the eyes of Runolf underneath his black hair. He thought of all the beatings he had received from this man, and he knew that if it were not for the use that Ketil had for Fiachra, Runolf would have been free to kill him long ago. Then he released the bow.

The arrow whistled through the air and buried itself deep in the head of the Norseman who pitched backwards into the trees with a terrible cry. In an instant his comrades had surrounded him. 'Runolf has been wounded!' was the first shout Fiachra heard. But as they bent over the fallen man, another shout pierced the air. 'He is dead, Lord Ketil!'

The tall Viking bent over the prone body of his son before the warriors around him picked up the lifeless body. The whole group disappeared quietly into the trees.

It was the last thing the defenders expected to happen, but only a few minutes elapsed before they could see that the invaders were moving. This time, it was possible to see what looked like small shafts of flame being carried by a few of the

Norsemen. When they reached the shore, it was clear that they were carrying narrow stakes of wood which they drove into the ground beneath them. The tops of the wood had been dipped in oil and each stake was set alight.

The islanders watched as the Viking archers strode forward in turn, their arrows already fitted to their bows, their tips wound with cloth. They set the material alight and fired the now-flaming bolts across the water towards the settlement. The burning arrows fell on the island like the rain that was now easing off. To Fiachra's surprise and alarm, despite the dampness of the buildings around them, a few of the shafts continued to burn and the flames began to spread.

Some of the women and older children helped the men fight the fires with the water they had collected. Fiachra was summoned to the wall along with the other archers. It was not easy to identify their opponents as the Vikings were behind the cover of trees. The Viking archers were firing at the easy targets provided by the buildings on the island, so they too were able to stand in the shadows with their comrades. Fiachra sent two of his arrows flying into the darkness before realising he was wasting his time.

He could see behind him that most of the flaming arrows had been put out although two buildings had caught fire. These were workshops, empty of people, but containing the work of the craftsmen on the island.

As the defenders continued to try to douse the fire, a shout was heard from one of the men on the fence. 'The crannog! The crannog is on fire!' Sure enough, as they looked across the water, the Norse arrows had reached the small man-made island. There were no people there to be hurt, but that meant there was no one there to stop the burning of the houses and the goods stored there. The settlers watched in anguish as much of what they had designed and crafted was destroyed before their eyes.

But this was not all. With a terrible cry, the Vikings attacked! Out from the trees emerged a huge tree trunk, shorn of its branches and carried aloft by six of the warriors. Dropping it to the ground, they began to push the timber. Soon they edged it out over the water, bridging the gap over the causeway and the men started to cross.

Fiachra and one of the others managed to hit two Norsemen, who stumbled onwards like drunk men, before falling heavily into the water beneath them. But more Vikings were crossing the makeshift bridge, and soon they were hammering at the door of the stockade with their axes. At the same time, the rest of the horde were negotiating the divide, balancing precariously on the fallen tree.

Inside the settlement directly behind the barred gate, Conaing, Fergus and Cathal stood with their swords drawn, along with half dozen of their men. Conaing urged the archers to fire without restraint. 'If any get through this gate we will be ready for them,' he said grimly. But even as he spoke the words, it was clear that the Norsemen would soon make their breakthrough.

The gate began to splinter, and a muscular arm appeared, pulling heavily on the shattered wood. Conaing rushed forward and his sword flashed down in an arc. The Viking screamed as the blade sliced clean through his arm. But the Norse axes were continuing their work on the other side of the gate and more of Ketil's men had reached the island.

Fiachra looked at the ground at his feet. There were no

more arrows left to fire. Once again, he thought that he had come to the end of his life. He moved away from the wall to join Conaing and the others in the open space behind the gate. If he were going to die in this fight he wanted to have a sword in his hand.

'There are no swords left,' said Conaing.

'Here! Take this.'

Cathal flung a spear towards him. Fiachra caught it in one hand. He was disappointed. With a spear he might, with a bit of luck, kill the first Norseman to confront him, but he knew that the weapon would be little use to him after that.

The Viking screams and shouts, and the sound of timber splitting and breaking, tearing and burning, had filled all ears for the last few minutes. But as the group of Scots stood defiantly in the open ground of the island, it seemed that the wind was bringing with it another sound. Moments later the Vikings, too, seemed to be aware of it.

One archer on the island wall shouted, 'It's Gabran's men!' At this, the defenders rushed over to the fence. Looking south they could see soldiers on horseback heading along the shore towards them. Each wore a metal helmet and carried a sword or spear, as well as a long shield. Some had the extra protection of chainmail.

As the horsemen drew nearer and began to charge at the group of Vikings still on the shore, most of the invaders turned to face them. At the same time, two of Ketil's men had forced their way through the door; they advanced towards the defenders. With gleaming eyes, they strode into the enclosure, swinging their battle axes. Fiachra, Conaing, Cathal and Fergus rushed to meet them.

Fiachra knew that he couldn't match the Vikings for

strength. He knew, too. that his spear would be of little use against an axe unless he struck quickly. Five paces away from the advancing Vikings, he threw his spear with all the strength he could gather to his arm. The tip of the weapon buried itself in the chest of his opponent and stopped him in his tracks. But the huge man didn't fall. Only a further thrust from the sword of Fergus brought him to the ground.

Fiachra looked around. A few paces beside them, Conaing and Cathal had killed the other man – but at a cost. A Norse axe had hit the leader of the villagers. Though he had been able to deflect some of the blow's force with his sword, Conaing now lay on the ground, blood seeping from a wound on his shoulder.

The defenders looked towards their gates and saw that no one else was arriving to continue the conflict. The rest of the Vikings had returned to the shore to deal with the new threat posed by the mounted soldiers. From the fence, Fiachra could see that the battle on the shoreline was well under way. The numbers were evenly matched and it was hard to see which side was gaining the upper hand. The Gaelic soldiers had the advantage of being on horseback, and their armour and mail protection was superior to the invaders' battledress. But the Vikings were experienced campaigners and ferocious in battle, and they were standing their ground. Fiachra could see Ketil and Gris striding through the fight wielding havoc with their terrible swords.

As he looked back along the shore, his beating heart accelerated even more. He could make out other riders some distance behind. One man, dressed in fine clothes, Fiachra recognised as Gabran, right hand man to the Gaelic chief of Dunadd, who stood watching the spectacle, surrounded by bodyguards. Though Gabran was middle aged and overweight, he was an experienced soldier. Fiachra could see a monk sitting on a white horse close to the water's edge. It was Breccan! And at his side, slightly further away from the island, there was the figure of a girl – a little taller than he remembered – but unmistakably Mor!

Fiachra tore his gaze away from these distant figures and looked once more at the battle taking place on the shore of the loch. He jumped down from his position on the fence and ran over to Conaing. The injured man was by this time propped up on one arm, his neck supported by Cathal. When Fiachra approached, he didn't move his head, but his eyes turned to meet those of the young man. 'I'll be alright, Fiachra,' he said. 'As long as we can win this day, my wounds will heal.'

'There's something we need to do,' said Fiachra. 'We need to leave here now and attack the Vikings.'

Conaing looked at him with surprise. 'We cannot leave here. This is the safest place.'

'The battle is not yet decided,' said Fiachra. 'It could go either way. But if we were to attack on another flank, the fight will turn in our favour.'

Cathal stared at the boy. 'If we leave this island to fight the Norse on the shore, some of our people here will die.'

'That may be,' admitted Fiachra. 'But others will be saved. If we don't help the soldiers out now we may lose everything.' He looked down at Conaing. 'Please order the people here to attack!'

'Who will lead them?'

'I will!' Fiachra stood up and looked around him. 'But I need a weapon.'

Conaing tried to lift himself up, and pulled Fiachra down to his level. Then he picked up the iron sword by his side. 'Take my sword. I have no use for it right now.' Fiachra stared at the weapon before taking it into his own hand. It was finely balanced, surprisingly wide at the hilt, and on its blade was inscribed INGELRII, the name of its maker.

'This is a Norse sword,' said Fiachra, with some surprise. 'And it's a good sword.'

'The Vikings make good swords.' Conaing smiled. 'Handle it well.'

As the fighting continued on the banks of the shore, Fiachra led the charge of the islanders. They burst through the splintered doors and carefully picked their way along the giant log that connected the island to the shore. In facing the Gaelic soldiers on the approach road on the shore, the Vikings had turned away from the island. Now some of them turned to face their new opponents. As Fiachra ran forwards, his mind was racing, wondering where this courage had come from. Was it because he had been so close to death? Or was it the presence of Breccan and Mor that gave him new hope?

Beside him were Cathal and Fergus; just behind were another eight men – hardly enough to defeat the Vikings alone, but perhaps enough to tip the balance. Fiachra wanted to head straight for Ketil, but the leader and Gris were fighting on the far side of the Viking group. Instead, his first task was to deal with the Norseman who now loomed in front of him. This Viking, armed with a sword, gave a howl of recognition as Fiachra moved towards him. The older man swung his sword through the air, aiming his blow at Fiachra's neck. What Fiachra lacked in strength, he made up for in speed. As he rushed forwards he ducked his head, avoiding the blow, but losing his footing; just before their bodies collided, he lunged forward with Conaing's sword. Both men fell to the ground; as Fiachra climbed back to his feet, he could see that the Norseman was dead.

The trees grew thickly in this part of the wood and it was hard to swing an axe or sword without connecting with timber. This meant that the horsemen were less effective in the density of the wood than they had been on open ground. But already a cry had been heard from Ketil and the invaders started to fall back and descend the hill towards their ship at Asknish.

Scarcely believing what had happened so quickly, Fiachra found himself stumbling forward and downward as the islanders and soldiers from Dunadd set off in pursuit. As he moved down the path, he became aware of a horse travelling beside him. He looked up at the soldier above him as he heard the voice, 'Who are you? Are you from the island?' The soldier was staring suspiciously at his clothes.

'My name is Fiachra. I'm from Ederline.'

The soldier looked more closely. 'Fiachra? Cuan's son. I remember you! You used to travel with your father. I've seen you before at Dunadd.' Then, ignoring the scar above Fiachra's eye, the man said tactfully, 'Your hair is longer.'

'I've been away for a while,' said Fiachra. The man reached down his arm, and pulled Fiachra up behind him on the horse. 'Come with me and we'll see the back of these Norsemen!' The horse-soldiers slowly made their way down the track towards Asknish, seemingly content to ensure that the Vikings left their land. The islanders, on foot now, turned back uphill towards Loch Glashan.

Fiachra could not wait to get back to the loch to see Mor and Breccan, but for now he continued the descent with the soldier, whose name was Aedan. An opening in the trees gave them a first glimpse of the village of Asknish, and Aedan reined in his horse so they could see what was happening. The light was all but gone, but the longship was clearly visible in the shallows of the bay. A body was being carefully lifted onto the boat by four Vikings, and Fiachra realised that it would be Runolf.

A few minutes later, more figures were seen moving out from the edge of the wood onto the beach. Aedan and Fiachra could see the striding figure of Ketil and the giant Gris by his side. As the last of the Vikings emerged from the undergrowth onto the shingly sand, the boat was pushed further out and the oars began to propel the craft into deeper water.

The ship was heading out to the open loch. Fiachra could hardly believe that Ketil was giving up so easily. At a rough count, it seemed that around twenty men had taken to the sea with their leader, but, even with so many losses, Ketil was not known as someone who would run from a fight.

Fiachra took a deep breath. He was home. The Vikings were on their way. And his friends were just a few minutes from him at the top of the hill. For the first time in many days, he could turn his attention to something positive.

There was the noise of a horse moving beside them, and as Aedan wheeled his horse to leave, another soldier joined them in the clearing. The two horses shook their heads together as if in greeting. The new rider looked across at Aedan. 'Let's pray we never see their Norse faces again.'

'Let's pray the ship goes down in a storm,' smiled Aedan.

93

As they set off up the slope, a shout rang out. It came from a soldier in the trees below. At first, it was impossible to identify the source of the alarm, but as they continued to gaze down to the waters of Loch Fyne, the cause of the cry was clear: Ketil's longship had rounded the point of the bay and was turning due south behind the wind. The open waters of the loch were almost black in the fading light. The large square mainsail was raised and, heading towards Ketil and the bay of Asknish, were four more ships. Their sails were dark but unmistakably square.

Fiachra felt his head swimming. These were Viking ships. It looked to him like the end of the world.

BIG PUZZLE

'You could have been killed!'

Mum announced this for the umpteenth time as they sped along the road towards Achnabreck. Bouncing along in the rear of the swaying car, Emma was tempted to mention that they were risking death by travelling so fast, but she knew it was better to keep quiet. Her Mum often drove quickly when she was angry, and she was angry now. She was also keen to get back to the cottage to see Aunt Isobel who had been dropped off at home after her visit to the hospital.

Ben sat in the front beside his mother. Having taken one of his boots off, his leg now stuck out straight in front of him. The ankle wasn't so painful now which was one of the reasons he decided to speak up on behalf of his older sister. He knew that she was the one Mum was blaming for their climb. 'My foot isn't too sore now, Mum. I don't think it's anything serious.'

'That's not the point!'

'But it *is* the point, Mum. The point is that I'm okay. And Emma helped me down safely.'

Katie shook her head. 'You should have known better, Emma. And Colin should have known better too. I mean, dropping you off at a museum that wasn't even open…'

'Well, how on earth was he to know?' asked Emma.

'He should have checked. He's a grown man.'

Emma was feeling bad but she could not see the point of blaming Colin. So she tried to change the subject. 'Tell me again what's wrong with Aunt Isobel?'

'She's got atrial fibrillation,' replied her Mum. 'That's according to the hospital after they gave her some tests.'

'But what is aerial tribulation?' asked Ben.

'It means she's got an irregular heartbeat. Her heart is beating too fast. It makes sense. It's why she's been feeling faint and having all those episodes of breathlessness.'

'So how does it get sorted?' asked Emma.

'She needs to start taking medication, and she needs to speak with her own doctor tomorrow morning.'

There was a silence in the car. Then Ben looked straight at his mother. 'Is she going to die?'

Katie smiled back. 'Don't worry. If she takes the medicine, she should be fine. And talking of tomorrow, Dad will be arriving in the afternoon.'

'That will be great,' said Ben. 'I've really been missing Dad.' Football at last, he thought.

As the car zipped along the road, Emma looked out at the field on her right. She could make out three standing stones at the furthest edge; she reckoned they were much taller than an adult. It was amazing to think that they had been here for thousands of years and people were still arguing over what they were and what they meant. Colin said that maybe the truth behind these stones would never be known.

But her heart was still racing with the excitement of discovering the slab on the hillside. There had to be a way of identifying what that carving meant. First on Emma's to-do list was to speak Colin. The children had already blurted out their find to their Mum but she didn't seem to be bothered. All that she seemed to want to do was to be angry that they had climbed a hill on their own, and without her permission.

When they arrived at the cottage Ben and Emma went straight into the living room to check on their Aunt. She was sitting in her usual chair. 'I'm alright, I think,' she said, 'I've to see my own doctor in the morning and he's going to give me some pills to take. But I'm not so breathless as I was when I woke up.'

'You will need to be very careful,' suggested Emma.

'Och, I'm not worried dearie,' said Isobel cheerfully. 'I've had plenty of pills before now.'

Mum was in the kitchen and they could hear the kettle boiling as Emma crossed over to the window. Immediately outside was the small back garden and the outhouse, but Emma was looking further up, beyond the fence and trees towards Colin's house. There was a space at the front driveway where his car was usually parked. From the kitchen came her mother's voice; as if she could predict what Emma was thinking. 'Colin isn't back yet.'

Ben sat on the sofa wiggling his toes, as his sister noisily sat down beside him. 'How's the foot?'

'It's not too bad. Still a bit sore but I think it might be okay in the morning.'

'I hope so,' said Emma. 'And I hope Colin gets home soon.'

'That Colin is an awful man!' Aunt Isobel was speaking to them from the other side of the room. 'Imagine telling you children stories about ghosts.'

Ben frowned. He had no idea what his Aunt was talking about. But Emma remembered. A few days before they had told the adults about their walk along the banks of the canal with Colin. 'He was telling us about the ghostly friars of Kilduskland,' she said, 'but he never said that he believed in the ghosts himself, Aunt Isobel. We're not frightened. Have *you* never heard these stories?'

'Never,' said Isobel, shaking her head, 'and I've lived here all my life.'

Emma looked over at the old woman. She suddenly felt that perhaps she might be able to help. 'Do you speak Gaelic, Aunt Isobel?'

'Not really. My husband Hector came from Lewis. He was a real Gaelic speaker. I never learned but I suppose I know a few words.'

Undaunted, Emma produced the notebook from the rucksack beside her. 'Do you know what 'Fiachra agus Mor' means?'

Isobel kept a silence for a while. She looked lost in thought and for a moment Emma imagined she was going to decipher the words. But then she said 'Agus means *and* in Gaelic.'

'So it's Fiachra *and* Mor,' she mused. That didn't help too much.

'But what does Fiachra mean? And what does Mor mean?'

'I think I may have heard the word 'Fiachra' before, but I don't know what it means.' Isobel paused for a few seconds.

'I think 'Mor' means 'big.''

Ben leaned nearer his sister, and spoke very quietly. 'That means the message is "something and big". That makes no sense at all.'

'You're right,' admitted Emma, as she flung herself back on the sofa. 'There is no sense in that.'

It was after dinner and well into the evening when they heard the noise of an engine; the headlights of a car shone into their cottage, scattering light and shadows across the walls. Emma and Ben looked to the window as Colin drove past but Mum was not going to allow them out tonight.

'Maybe you can see Colin in the morning, but not now. Ben, we'll see how your foot is after a night's sleep. And Emma, after your performance today, you can have an early night as well.' Emma groaned. Mum's mood wasn't softening.

As Ben settled into his bed, Emma lay across from him on top of hers, surrounded by the maps, leaflets and books that Colin had let them borrow. They opened the books first but they found them too hard to understand. Eventually Emma started to study an Ordnance Survey map of the area. It occurred to her that the words could be the names of places. The more she looked at the map, the more she became aware of the strangest names like *Rhudil*, *Tibertich* and *Lechuary*.

With crazy names like these on the map, Emma began to think it would only be a matter of time before a word like *Fiachra* would appear. But it was something else that caused her to sit straight up on the bed. 'I've found it!' she announced.

'Found what?'

'It's been right in front of my face. The whole area around Dunadd is called Moine Mhor.' Emma dropped the map and began to work her way through the items on her bed until she reached the brochure that she had remembered. For a moment she was silent. Then she looked over to her brother. 'It means the 'Great Moss'.'

'So Mor means Moss?' said Ben.

'It looks like it,' nodded Emma. She was feeling very pleased with herself. 'Aunt Isobel was wrong. The whole land around Dunadd and Kilmartin is a big area of bog. That's what 'moss' means. It all makes sense.'

But Ben was not impressed. 'Are you serious? Now you are saying that the message is '*Something* and Moss.' And you think *that* makes sense?'

Emma let out a sigh. Ben was right. 'We really need to speak to Colin,' she said, clearing the top of her duvet and pulling pyjamas from under her pillow. She climbed into bed and switched off the lamp beside her. The room was instantly dark. 'It'll be good to see Dad tomorrow.'

Ben grunted a quiet 'Yes' in reply. He was almost asleep.

THE SWORD

Ketil was no coward but he needed some time to regroup his men – and his thoughts. For a Viking to fall in battle was an honourable way to die – it was even seen as glorious, leading to an afterlife in Valhalla. Like all Norse warriors he was ready to die with a sword in his hand.

But first, he needed a plan. For what consumed his mind now was the need for vengeance. He had one desire above all else – to wreak his revenge on Fiachra, who had betrayed him, and whose actions had led to the death of his men and his son. He could scarcely believe that this was Runolf now, lying stretched out, lifeless on the deck at his feet. To add to his anger, some of his soldiers were saying they had seen Fiachra himself firing the fatal arrow.

As the ship rounded the point of the bay and moved from the calm waters of Loch Gair to the deeper swell of Loch Fyne, Ketil stooped over the dead body of his son. As he crouched down, his own body shook with grief and rage and he prayed to the gods to help him. It was Gris, his other son, who got his attention by placing a hand on his father's shoulder. 'Father – look ahead.' As Ketil stood up and looked beyond the bow of the longship, the other vessels were nearly upon them. There were four ships, unmistakably Norse, heading towards them and the square mainsail on the leading galley seemed familiar to him.

'I know that ship,' he said. At his side Gris nodded his head in agreement.

'It looks like Ragnar.'

'I've not seen Ragnar for some time,' said Ketil. His temper began to recede as he took in the situation in front of him. It seemed that the gods were quick in answering his prayer! Ketil barked out an order and the oars were pulled in on one side of his warship. The oars on the other ship were likewise withdrawn and the two longships met in the middle of the loch. As they drew together, Ketil stepped across onto the other boat, calling on Gris to follow him.

Ragnar was clad in chainmail as befitted a chieftain, though his head was bare. A heavy cloak hung from his shoulders. A wide smile flashed through his thick black beard as he stepped forward to greet his old friend. Ketil moved forward to embrace his comrade, his eyes already looking beyond him to examine the ship he had boarded.

This warship was much bigger than his own. Along each side of the decking sat the rowers. There were no benches on a longship; each warrior sat on a wooden chest which contained his personal belongings. Ketil noted that there were many unoccupied chests. Clearly this ship had lost some of its crew.

'Ketil, I have been looking for you. It is good to see you,' said Ragnar, stealing a glance over to the shore. 'It seems you are leaving in a hurry?'

'It seems you have had trouble of your own,' countered Ketil, glancing over Rangar's shoulder at the empty spaces behind him. 'The last I heard, you were fighting with the King on one of his campaigns.'

'This campaign will be the last,' said Ragnar.

'How so?'

'Because the King is dead!'

As Ketil and Gris digested this news, Ragnar led them to the rear of the ship, and they sat down beside him. A short length of sail was stretched above their heads, creating a makeshift canopy and shelter. Ketil asked Ragnar to explain.

'We were fighting with the King in Ireland and we won all our battles until the end. Magnus sent ahead for supplies for the voyage home before he decided to lead us through a marsh on our way to the coast.' Ragnar saw the look on the faces of Ketil and Gris. 'He thought it would be a shortcut, but it was like a swamp. There we were ambushed and many died – including the King himself. Now those of us who made it back to the ships have the task of returning to Norway without our King.'

'You didn't recover his body?' asked Ketil.

'We were unprepared for the attack; we were taken completely by surprise. The King still lies where he fell.' Ragnar paused, then shouted to one of his men. 'Rorick!' A tall Norseman strode along the deck towards the three men, his long blonde hair billowing out behind him. 'Get the sword.'

The slim man sprang down from the deck and disappeared under the storage area for a few moments. He emerged, carrying what looked like a sword wrapped in cloth. When he reached Ketil and Gris he began to unveil the weapon, slowly and reverently, as if it were a sacred relic. 'We did not recover the King himself,' said Ragnar. 'But we have his sword!'

The two visitors gazed in awe as Ragnar pulled the weapon from its jewel-encrusted scabbard and laid it on the cloth. The blade shone despite the fading light around them, and the pommel at the top of the handgrip was inlaid with gleaming white ivory. The handgrip itself was thick and wound with gold thread. Ketil couldn't help himself. He reached forward and took the sword up in his hand. It was heavy, but nicely balanced. 'So this is Legbiter,' he said.

'And I have been charged to take it back to the court in Norway,' said Ragnar. 'But I have made a little detour to come here to find you.'

'How did you know where I was?' asked Ketil, reluctantly handing the sword back to Rorick.

'I didn't know for sure but I heard a rumour that you were back raiding in Alba, and I know these waters are among your favourites.'

'What can I do to help you?' asked Ketil.

'It is I who am trying to help *you*,' said Ragnar. 'I want to give you a chance to redeem yourself.'

'What do you mean?'

'Everyone knows that before Magnus became king you were loyal to his rival, Haakon, and that even after Haakon died you still did nothing to support Magnus. The King sometimes spoke about you, and said that when he returned he would see to it that you were punished for not supplying a longship for his navy. Now that he is dead, that won't happen. The wife of Magnus has not given him a child. But there will be a new king eventually who will have to decide who should be punished for this defeat.'

'What are you trying to say, Ragnar?'

'If you come with me back to Norway, I will say that you have helped in the campaign. I will stop any charges being made against you, and together we will swear fealty to a new king. There is no need for you to continue to live like an outlaw.'

'Why would you do this?'

'We were friends before. We were friends when we were growing up. It would be good to be friends again. Come with me, Ketil. Together we can take the King's sword back to where it belongs.' Ketil's face didn't move. Nor did his expression change. He continued to gaze down at the wooden planks beneath him. Gris sat staring at his father, until the older man finally began to speak.

'Very well. Thank you for remembering me. I *will* come with you,' he said. 'But first I need your help, for I have business to finish here.'

Ragnar snorted in disgust and with a wave of his hand, dismissed the land around them. 'Forget this place. Alba doesn't matter. We need to return home.'

Ketil spoke again. His head remained bowed, as his eyes continued to fix themselves on the deck. 'This is a matter of honour,' he said, 'our group was betrayed by one of my slaves, a boy I took from these lands three years ago. Now my son Runolf lies dead, shot by this traitor. Before I leave here I must see justice done. I must have revenge.'

Ragnar rose to his feet. 'What is it you want me to do?'

Ketil stood up beside him and cast an eye over to the

105

other boats on the loch. 'How many men do you have?'

'There are about one hundred and seventy of us,' replied Ragnar.

'We have twenty-three. Together we have nearly two hundred warriors,' said Ketil, 'we must avenge the deaths of our countrymen.'

'We have no time for this. We have to get home with the sword. My men have been fighting for months.'

Ketil extended his arm and pointed to the nearest hills. 'This will take little time. The boy Fiachra is skulking on an island less than two miles away, surrounded by old men and women and children. They will be easy pickings for us.'

'Easy pickings? Then why did you not finish him off yourself?' asked Ragnar.

'Some soldiers of the Gaels ambushed us and drove us back to the shore. But now we easily outnumber them. Come with me till I get Fiachra, and then I will follow you and the sword back to Norway.' Ragnar continued to hesitate. 'Do you remember Ubbe? He is dead. And Bolli? He is dead. And Olaf the Bear, and Runolf – my son.'

Ketil grabbed at the arm of his comrade. 'We must honour these men by avenging their deaths. It is our duty. You say you want me to be part of a united Norway where people support each other? Right here is the place to start! We begin by avenging the deaths of our brothers who have been killed by treachery!'

Ragnar moved over to Rorick and mumbled quietly to him. Then, without speaking, Rorick started signalling to the men in the boats. Oars were manoeuvred into the water and the five Norse ships began the silent journey to Asknish.

FIACHRA AND MOR

When Aedan and Fiachra arrived back at the shores of the settlement, the news of the returning Norse ships had already reached the defenders. Springing down from the horse, Fiachra's first hope was to see Mor but there was no sign of her on the banks of the loch. So he crossed over the causeway to the island, noting that the islanders' bridge had been put back in place. Moving through the gateway, the first person he saw was Gabran. Mounted on his horse, he towered over those around him. He was speaking to Conaing who had managed to rise to his feet, though he was leaning against a wall for support. Cathal and Fergus stood by his side.

'Staying here is no longer the safest thing. We need to leave the island. Everyone needs to make their way down to Dunadd. Only there can safety be assured.'

'We are grateful for your help Gabran. But we have old people here,' said Conaing. 'And some of us are wounded,' he added bitterly.

'Listen! Gabran is right, Conaing,' said Cathal. 'We cannot stay here any longer. We cannot defend this island against the enemies at the loch below us. When they return here we will be no match for them.' Gabran continued, 'I've given instructions to some of my soldiers to give up their horses to help transport the wounded and the old people down the path. These soldiers will walk with them. We will all walk together. But everyone must take only what they can easily carry.'

Fiachra understood the route they were proposing. They would go over the hills at the western part of the loch and take the downhill trail which followed the River Add. That path would take them to the church and the village of Kilmichael. From there it was less than one mile to the ancient fort, which was once the capital of the kingdom.

Conaing spotted Fiachra standing on the muddy grass. He looked up to Gabran. 'This boy has acted as a hero today. This is Fiachra, the son of Cuan.' Gabran turned to look at the young man in front of him.

'I remember you, and I remember your father. But I thought you had both been killed?'

'There is a long story there,' said Fiachra. 'The Vikings took me as their prisoner but I have now returned.'

'So we see,' said Gabran. He smiled. Then he continued to give orders to bring about the departure from the island.

Fiachra moved through the settlement, bending low to stare into each building. People were moving out from the island, clutching possessions in their hands. As he watched, the cattle and a few pigs were herded out towards the bridge. Then he saw Etain, and as he went towards her she caught sight of him. The older woman spoke first. 'Fiachra! You are not hurt?'

'I am not hurt, Etain, thank God. Have you seen Mor?'

Etain smiled. 'Yes I have. And I have told her that you are alive. She is looking for you by the shore.'

'Thanks Etain,' shouted Fiachra, as he began to run towards the bridge.

As soon as he set foot on the banks of the loch he saw her. She was helping a young man onto his horse. The youth was nursing a wound on his shoulder which made it hard for him to balance on the animal. Once he had settled himself properly into the saddle, the girl started to look around again.

'Mor! Mor!' Suddenly Fiachra was there, running towards her. She squealed with delight to see him.

'Fiachra!'

And then she was in his arms. He was finally holding her in his arms as he had always wanted to do.

'It's so great to see you, Mor,' he whispered.

She took a step backwards but kept holding on to the sleeves on his tunic. 'Everyone said you were dead. Nobody knew. I prayed you were alive, but I wasn't sure I would ever see you again.'

As Mor spoke to him, Fiachra looked at her face. The dark curls were still there, as was the sparkle in her eyes when she smiled. She had changed only a little, yet she seemed more a woman than a girl. Mor had never looked finer.

'Look at you!' he said, laughing.

'Look at *you*!' Mor replied.

Her fingers began touching his face and for a moment she

traced along the deep scar on his forehead. 'This is what they did to you?' she asked. Fiachra nodded. Sensing his embarrassment, Mor smiled, 'Your hair is so long now and you look so grown up. And look at your clothes!'

Fiachra grinned back at her. He had never felt so happy. For three years Fiachra had been dreaming of this day. Here he was in front of her at last and now he didn't know what to say. It seemed Mor felt the same. They stood gazing at each other.

The moment was broken by some islanders jostling against Fiachra as they attempted to move past him. Then Fiachra understood he was standing on the path, blocking the way, and all around him people were trying to begin their journey. Mor spoke. 'Let me go back to Etain and see if she needs any help. Then I will join you on the trail.'

Fiachra remembered the sword that was tucked into his belt. 'I also have something to do. I'll see you soon.'

Conaing was now approaching on horseback, having crossed over the bridge. As Conaing drew near, Fiachra stepped out in front of the animal. He lifted the sword up towards the chieftain. 'Here is your sword, Conaing. Thank you for lending it to me.'

Conaing bent forward to be nearer Fiachra, but did not reach out for the sword. 'I hear you fought like a lion today.'

Fiachra felt his face redden. 'I think many fought bravely today.'

Then Conaing sat upright, tugging at the belt around his waist. 'I will have no need of this sword for some time. I give it to you for now.' And he handed the belt and empty scabbard to the younger man.

'This is an honour,' replied Fiachra. He knew it was no

small thing to be given a sword – especially one so finely made. 'I will look after it,' he said solemnly.

'Pray God you don't have to use it again,' said Conaing, urging his horse forward on the path.

As the islanders made their way around the shore of the loch, they cast their eyes back to the island and the crannog they were abandoning. Since these homes and workshops would now be undefended, it seemed certain that they would end up being destroyed.

Fiachra walked slowly down the trail. It was not long before Etain and Mor caught up with him. Each was carrying a bundle of clothes and bags. As Fiachra had nothing to carry, he took Etain's possessions into his own arms. There was another man walking alongside the women, carrying a bundle of leather goods and animal hides. As Fiachra looked more closely at him, Etain made the introduction. 'This is my husband, Dallin,' she said.

The big man beside her leaned over to grasp Fiachra's arm. He was wearing a leather waistcoat of similar style to Cathal's. It occurred to Fiachra that the items he was carrying had been salvaged from the workshops on the crannog. 'I am pleased to meet you. I remember your father well.'

Fiachra smiled to himself. He wondered if he would ever be as famous as his father. There was a mile to travel through the oaks on the western edge of the loch before they reached the River Add. As they walked through the substantial trees, Fiachra shuddered to imagine how many longships the Vikings could make out of the wood.

Gabran, or one of his soldiers, was riding up and down beside the retreating group, constantly urging them to move

111

more quickly. Should the Vikings return this evening and set off in pursuit, it would be a race to reach the safety of Dunadd. By the time they came to the river and began their descent, the light was fading. If they got to the fortress at all it would be in the darkness.

Fiachra turned to Mor. 'Where is Breccan? I saw him before. But I can't see him here.'

'He has gone ahead with two soldiers to tell Lochlann what has happened and to prepare Dunadd for our arrival.'

'I was really hoping to see him here,' admitted Fiachra.

'He didn't really want to go,' said Mor. 'He got into an argument with Gabran. He was determined to bury those who were killed today. But Gabran wouldn't hear of it. He said it was too dangerous; there wasn't time – and he told him to do something more useful.' Mor reached over and took Fiachra's arm. 'Don't worry. You'll see him tonight at Dunadd.'

Then she leaned close to him. 'I can't talk to you properly with all these people around us. Let's meet tonight. I want to speak with you and hear all that has happened to you.'

'It will be very late by the time we reach Dunadd,' said Fiachra.

Mor looked into his eyes. 'I don't care.'

Fiachra nodded and grinned. 'Neither do I!'

Gabran had left two Gaels back at the loch. Their job was to keep a lookout on the Vikings. The other cavalrymen had the job of encouraging the travellers to move as swiftly as possible without allowing the group to become too stretched out. Should the Vikings manage to pursue them, their only hope was to stand together.

The path led downhill to the floor of the neighbouring

glen. After that, the terrain was more open and the ground flatter. It was only a mile or so to Kilmichael with its church and cluster of houses and huts but there were no defences there. Beyond Kilmichael lay the vast expanse of Crinan Moss and the fortress of Dunadd perched high upon a hill. The rock rose out of the bog like a whale rising out of the sea, and the fort was visible for miles in all directions. But as darkness was falling, the little band had to rely on their memory to guide them forward.

As they stumbled into Kilmichael, there was no sound to greet them. It took a few moments to realise that the villagers had gone – and they had left in a hurry. Breccan and the soldiers must have encouraged them to seek safety in the walls of the fort.

There was a well beside the church, and some of the travellers had stopped for water. Many were feeling weary and asked Gabran for a time of rest. But the soldier in charge of the troops urged them back to their feet and Conaing agreed with him. Now that he had taken the decision to leave the island he was anxious to reach safety without delay.

Ahead of them in the darkness lay the Great Moss; the trail across the bog needed to be followed closely. Just as the group began to focus on the next stage of their journey, a noise was heard from the opposite direction. It was the sound of horses moving quickly, heading towards them. 'That must be the soldiers that were left back at the loch,' said Fiachra to Mor as they peered into the darkness.

Gabran moved his horse to the end of the procession. He signalled towards Conaing. 'Come with me. My men are bringing a message,' he said.

113

But Conaing remained motionless. 'We don't need to hear the message,' he said. 'We know what they are going to say.' Conaing lifted his arm and pointed a finger to the hills behind them. Above the darkness of the trees and bushes around them, and above the featureless black of the hills, there was a little purple moonlight in the sky. As the company gazed, curls of smoke were visible billowing up into the night air.

Everyone knew what this meant. In the darkness, beside Fiachra and Mor, a man spoke out. 'They are burning our homes.'

COLIN'S STORIES

When Ben woke up, Emma was sitting on her bed. She was wearing green leggings and an extremely long Aran jumper that Isobel had knitted a few years ago, which finally fitted Emma – as a dress. She also had her red anorak zipped up to her neck and a beanie on her head. These items, plus the wellington boots on her feet, suggested to a still groggy Ben that she was ready to go out – and that the weather was not good. 'Why are you up so early?' he asked.

'It's not early. It's nine thirty. You've been asleep for ages.'

Ben turned to the clock at the side of his bed. Emma was right. 'You look like a gnome,' he said. A pillow flew across the room towards him with all the force Emma could muster. Ben sat up straight, looking for something to retaliate with.

But before war broke out between them, Emma spoke. 'Colin is in. I've just seen him out in the garden. We should go and see him soon in case he goes out.'

'What about my breakfast?'

'I thought you wanted to see him quickly,' said Emma. Ben pulled back the bed covers.

'You're right. Give me a minute to get ready.'

A sudden noise made both children jump and turn towards the window. A fierce shower of rain rattled the wooden frame and shook the glass. 'The weather isn't getting any better,' said Emma grimly.

Aunt Isobel seemed in better form as she sat chatting with their Mum. Ben took a piece of toast from the breakfast table and headed for the door with Emma at his heels. 'Where are you two going so fast? Ben, you've only just got up.'

'We're just going up to Colin's house, Mum. We want to catch him in case he has to go out.'

'Well, don't stay up there too long. I'm taking Aunt Isobel to the doctor later this morning and we must make sure that someone is around when Dad gets here.'

Ben turned to his mother 'When is that?'

'He should be here about twelve, I think.'

'Don't worry about that,' said Emma, waving. 'We'll be back long before that. Good luck with the doctor, Aunt Isobel.'

The two children filed outside. The sky was black overhead and the rain relentless as they trudged up the slope towards the house. 'How is that foot of yours this morning, anyway?' asked Emma, as she noticed Ben sliding on the stone slabs in front of Colin's door.

'It's pretty good,' replied Ben. 'Just don't ask me to climb another hill today.'

Emma stole a glance at the dark clouds above them.

'There's not much chance of that,' she said.

Colin welcomed them inside and brought them into his sitting room. He collapsed into his seat with a hot drink while Emma and Ben looked around for somewhere they might sit down. 'So, what's your news?' asked the big man.

'Well, today we really do have some news for you,' said Emma. 'Remember when you dropped us off at Kilmartin yesterday?' Colin nodded. 'Well, it was shut for the day. Something to do with repairs ... so Ben and I decided to climb a hill. We went up Beinn Bhan.'

'That's quite a hill to climb by yourself,' said Colin, raising his eyebrows.

Ben joined in the conversation, 'That's what Mum said.'

'But anyway, we went up the hill to see St Breccan's Cell.'

Colin smiled broadly. 'Great view from up there. Didn't I tell you?'

'Yes, you did. It *was* a good view. But listen to this! When we were up there, we – I mean Ben really – discovered a stone that was hidden in the ground. It was like a gravestone – or even an old milestone – that's been overgrown by grass and heather.'

'And there was writing on the stone,' said Ben.

'But we don't know what the writing means,' said Emma.

'I'm not surprised,' said Colin, taking a sip from his drink. He looked over at the children. 'If a stone is old it's usually hard to read whatever has been carved on it. The words and symbols get eroded by the weather.'

'But we *do* know what it says. I copied it down here in my notebook. It's just that we don't understand what the words mean. The stone reads "Fiachra agus Mor".'

Colin nearly dropped the coffee in his hand. 'What did you say?'

'Fiachra agus Mor.'

As the children looked over at their neighbour, they saw his eyes widen and his mouth hang open. 'Fiachra agus Mor ...' repeated Colin, 'who's been telling you about them?'

'Them?' asked Ben. 'We don't know what the words mean.'

'But we know that *Mor* means bog,' said Emma confidently.

Colin looked at her quizzically. '*Mor* means bog?'

'Yes!' she said. 'I looked it up in one of your books. The area around Kilmartin and Dunadd is called the Moine Mhor which means the Great Moss. So *Mor* means moss or bog. That's all we know for sure.'

Colin extended his hand to Emma. 'Show me the words in your notebook.' Emma leafed through the book to the last page and handed it over. He sat quietly, staring at the words, not speaking or moving. Ben and Emma thought it strange that he could take so long to read three small words.

Finally he opened his mouth. 'Emma, you have the words in the wrong order. The word for moss is *Moine*. Mhor is the word for *great* or *big*.'

The children looked at each other. 'Aunt Isobel was right after all,' said Ben.

'But this word *Mor* in your carving is spelled without an "h",' continued Colin. 'It's a person's name. So is *Fiachra*.'

'So this has got nothing to do with a bog or moss?' said Emma. '*Fiachra* and *Mor* are the names of two people?'

Colin nodded slowly. He still looked deep in thought. 'But this is just amazing.'

Emma couldn't stand it any longer. 'Please Colin, tell us what it is that is so amazing. What is so amazing about a stone with two names on it?'

'Okay,' he said, running his hands through his beard and trying to concentrate his attention on Ben and Emma, who were sitting so patiently waiting for an answer, 'let me tell you what is so amazing about Fiachra and Mor.' Just as he seemed to be about to continue, he stood up and began walking away from the children. 'But first I need to boil the kettle again.'

At last Colin wandered back through to the sitting room, carrying a tray. He had poured some Coke for Emma and Ben and made fresh coffee for himself. There were chocolate biscuits piled high on a plate. It was still early in the day but with no Mum here to stop them, the children were quick to help themselves.

'Fiachra and Mor,' Colin began, 'lived right here, nine hundred years ago.'

'In this house?' asked Ben.

Emma glared across at him, but Colin simply laughed. 'My house isn't *that* old!'

'I was just joking,' said Ben. But he could feel his face going red.

'What I mean is that they lived in this area. Fiachra came from a few miles north of here near a loch called Ederline, and Mor came from Asknish, which is where the village of Loch Gair is today.'

'Where you keep your boat,' said Ben.

'Where I *used* to keep my boat,' corrected Colin.

'Anyway, they lived here a long time ago.'

'Were they kings or chiefs?' asked Emma.

'Or Vikings?' Ben added.

'They were Gaels – descendants of the Kingdom of Dalriada. They weren't kings or chiefs and they weren't Vikings, but they lived at the time of the Vikings. In fact they stood up for the people here against the Norse attacks.'

'What is the Kingdom of Dalriada?' asked Emma. Ben turned towards his sister.

'Colin told us about Dalriada when we went to Dunadd,' he said. Then he remembered that Emma hadn't been with them that day.

'Where we are right now was once the Gaelic kingdom of Dalriada and the hilltop fort of Dunadd was the centre. The simplest way to think of it is that this place was once the ancient capital of Scotland.'

Emma decided to get the conversation back on track. 'You still haven't told us what is so strange about these two men – Fiachra and Mor. Were they soldiers?'

'They weren't actually men. When their story begins Fiachra and Mor were a boy and girl, not much older than you too. But that's just it! This is what is so strange for me. The story of Fiachra and Mor has been handed down for years. My grandfather told it to me when I was really small. But nobody knew that the stories were real. They were just stories. But now ...' Colin's voice trailed off.

Ben encouraged him to say more. 'But now ... what?'

'Well if this stone is real, it could mean that Fiachra and Mor were real too. It means that the legends about them may well be true after all.'

'So what are the legends?' asked Emma.

'Well the story I was told was that when Fiachra was a young boy he saw Magnus Barefoot drag his boat across the land at Tarbert. Remember the fridge magnet you found? Fiachra and Mor were great friends and one day at Asknish there was a Viking raid by a Norse pirate called Ketil the Cruel. Fiachra happened to be there with Mor when the raid took place. Everyone was killed in the attack, including their parents, but Fiachra saved Mor's life by hiding her. Then he was taken prisoner by the Vikings. They took him to Norway and he was kept as a slave for three years. Ketil brought Fiachra back to Scotland because he wanted him to help them on their Scottish raids. None of his men could speak Gaelic, so having Fiachra was useful.'

'So he used Fiachra to betray his own people,' said Ben.

'That was his plan,' admitted Colin. 'But they sailed back to Asknish once more and instead of helping them, Fiachra led the Vikings along the wrong path. Then he made his escape and found his way to an island in Loch Glashan. Have you heard of Loch Glashan?' The two children shook their heads. 'It's in the hills above Loch Gair. There was a terrible battle which the Scots won. Fiachra was one of the heroes; he killed one of Ketil's sons.'

'And Fiachra is the same age as me?' said Emma.

Colin smiled. 'Not quite. By that time he would have been about seventeen. Mor was the same age.

Ben sat up in his seat. 'Is that the end of the story?'

Colin looked down at his watch. 'It certainly isn't, but the rest can wait. You need to get yourselves back down to your Aunt Isobel's if you're going to be there for your Dad arriving.'

'What about the stone?'

'Well the first thing we need to do is to see it properly. You can take me there and I'll have a look at it.' Colin walked them over to the door. 'Tell your Dad about it when he arrives. Maybe he can come with us.'

As the children walked quickly down the path, Colin shut his door to keep out the driving rain. Then he crossed the room to the table where the children had been sitting. He bent down to pick up the empty glasses and then stared in amazement at the plate he had given to the children.

The biscuits were gone.

DARKNESS

In the distance, lights flickered along the walls of Dunadd as the group of assorted Gaels followed the track across The Moss and drew near to the fort. The lights acted both as a welcome sight and a guide, and as they approached, they could see the huge gates open to receive them with a group of soldiers standing at the entrance. Above these men, the lights reflected on the spears of those who were patrolling the battlements. Fiachra turned to look behind him, but there was nothing there except silence and darkness. It was clear that they had made it to the safety of the fortress.

The black hill loomed above them, rising out of the flatness of the surrounding ground. At one time, the building here had been a much smaller fort, made out of stone and timber, and forming a circle around the summit of the mound. Over the years it had been added to, and now it covered a much greater area. There was an inner and an outer wall, and a whole community of houses, stables and workshops was clustered inside the enclosure around a Great Hall.

The fortress of Dunadd had never been bigger, yet Fiachra knew from stories told to him by his parents, that it was not the place it had once been – the home of kings and the capital of the Gaelic Kingdom of Dalriada. Once coronations had taken place on this hill, and royalty had been entertained with feasts and festivals. Markets were still held regularly, and it remained a trading centre, but the foreign merchants who used to often sail their boats up to Crinan were seen much less frequently these days, as the Kings of Alba were now treating Scone as the new capital of the country. Instead of being at the heart of the kingdom, Dunadd now had become an outpost on the frontier – a place to defend against the Norsemen, whose raiding and settlements were making much of the west coast into a new Norway.

Gabran led the way through its gates, followed by his mounted soldiers and the injured and elderly villagers who had been given horses to help them on their journey. Behind the horses trooped the rest of the weary company on foot. Like everyone around him, Fiachra felt exhausted and grateful for the safety of Dunadd's walls.

Once everyone was inside the fort, the large gates were pulled shut and bolted. As they stood inside the first – and largest – enclosure, Fiachra smiled at Mor and looked around at the occupants of the fort. He was hoping to see Breccan. But the visitors were being escorted further in, through smaller gates in the inner wall to where the Great Hall was located. From there came the smell of fires and cooking and the noise of many people talking as they all crowded into the building.

Outside the main entrance stood a man with folded arms, looking out at the new arrivals as they filed past him. His long robe appeared nearly white in the darkness, and his grey hair reached almost to his waist. His face was lined with age, and though he was trying to appear calm, his darting eyes and the furrows on his brow suggested anxiousness.

Fiachra recognised Lochlann, the man appointed by the King to be the keeper of the fort. He didn't appear to have changed at all in the three years since Fiachra had last seen him. When everyone was inside the hall, Lochlann made his entrance and sat on a large seat at the head of the room. The seat was ornate and raised above the ground. To Fiachra it looked like a throne; he wondered if it had actually been a throne in a past time.

The old man stood up to address the assembled group. 'This has been a black day. But you are all welcome here. Together we are strong and safe in this fortress. There is no sign of the Norsemen but even if they come here, we can defend this place. I have already sent out for reinforcements.' Lochlan spoke out loudly and confidently. He called for food to be served, and people began to take their places around the long tables.

Gabran sat next to the chief and continued to tell him about the battle at the loch. As he sat down to eat, Fiachra heard Etain and Dallin invite Mor to join them; they stood for a short time in the shadows talking with a family who lived in the fort. Many of the people at Loch Glashan were friends or relations of those at Dunadd. When Mor returned, she told Fiachra that friends of her family had offered them accommodation.

'It means that you will need to sleep here in the hall with

the others. Dallin says I must stay with them tonight.'

'I'll see you in the morning,' said Fiachra.

'The morning's not soon enough,' replied Mor, 'I want to see you later, as soon as the meal is over. Let's meet above here, beside the coronation stone.'

Fiachra nodded as Mor started to move out of the Great Hall. She had hardly disappeared from sight before a new figure stepped through the doorway into the lighted room. It was Breccan. The two men embraced before Breccan said, 'It is wonderful to see you, Fiachra. My prayers have been answered. God has protected you.'

The younger man looked into the serene and kindly eyes of his old friend. If Lochlann's eyes were filled with consternation, Breccan's eyes were filled with calm and peace. 'I am so glad to see you,' admitted Fiachra. 'The whole time I was in Norway I dreamed I would see you again – and Mor.'

'Mor will be so pleased to know you are safe. You have seen her?'

'Yes, I have seen her. She has gone down near the main gate to stay with some family friends.'

Breccan swung a leg over the bench and sat down beside Fiachra. 'Then you have some time. I must hear your story', he said.

Time wore on; those who had no relations or friends to join started to bed down for the night in the Great Hall. Fiachra said a farewell to Breccan and climbed the short stairway to reach the topmost point of the fortress. Here on a small plateau was a large stone where the image of a boar had been carved, and a footprint gouged into the rock. Years before, Kings had stood in this spot for their coronation.

Right now the place was silent and dark but Fiachra was not alone. Sentries were keeping watch, both westwards towards the sea and, especially tonight, towards the darkness in the east – the direction in which he had already come.

After a few minutes a smaller figure came through the inner gates and moved past the hall, drawing near to the stairway. The hood of her cloak was pulled over her head, and the material was wrapped around her body against the chill evening air, as Mor began to climb up to where Fiachra was sitting. As he gazed down at her, Fiachra remembered the last day in Asknish before the attack and how she had climbed up the rocks to meet him then. She sat down beside him in the darkness. The cloak disguised her shape, making her look like a monk, but Mor threw the hood back and shook out her curly hair before she smiled over at Fiachra. 'So tell me,' she said. 'Tell me everything that's happened to you.'

For Fiachra, there was no way to be sure how long he sat there with Mor that night as they exchanged their stories. There were soldiers moving past them on their lookout duty, but no one else was around.

Immediately below was the Great Hall, the biggest building in the fort, and despite being filled with unexpected visitors it was strangely quiet, as everyone tried to sleep. Beyond the hall, the inner wall led to the bigger courtyard beyond and the main entrance. Here were the stables, the workshops and the houses of those who lived permanently in the castle. Somewhere down there in the darkness was where Mor would sleep tonight.

As he had entered the fortress, Fiachra had noticed a leather workshop that he had visited more than once before

127

with his father though he could not remember the names of the people who worked there. He knew that some pottery was made here and that there was a big metal workshop which produced everything from large tools and weapons to small brooches. Some of the brooches were commissioned by royalty; the metal pins inlaid with amber that held the cloaks of Conaing and Lochlann were gifts from the King in thanks for their service.

Fiachra told Mor of his time in exile and his yearning to be home, and Mor described how she had waited on that terrible day for Fiachra to return. Eventually she had decided to crawl out of her hiding place to find that everyone had been killed and her village destroyed. Asknish was deserted and the Vikings were gone; it wasn't long before some of the men from Loch Glashan came down the hill. They saw her safely to Etain, her aunt, who lived on the crannog with her new husband Dallin. And so Mor came to live on the loch. 'It was all such a nightmare – so many good people killed.'

Fiarchra nodded at Mor's words, but could not say anything. With the death of Preddan and Orlaith, Mor had lost both her parents. With the death of Cuan he, himself, had lost his only living parent. As Mor had related her story he had been reliving the horror of that day in his memory.

Finally he said, 'I thought that maybe everyone died that day. I thought that maybe you would have been discovered too. I prayed that you would escape.' A gust of wind sent a chill through them as they sat together in the darkness, and Fiachra carefully put his arm around the girl. They sat there for a long time without moving or speaking until Mor broke the silence.

'Dallin says it's time I got married,' said Mor.

'And what do you say to that?'

'Well there is someone who is interested – his name is Conall. He lives at Ardifuir.'

Fiachra felt himself freeze at these words. He tried to speak without showing any emotion. The words came out slowly. 'And so, you *like* this Conall?'

'Not really. I don't care for him much. Dallin and Etain say he would make a good husband, but I want to marry someone I love.'

'That's a good idea,' admitted Fiachra, starting to relax once more. She turned towards him and smiled.

'It has been wonderful to see you today, even though the day has also been so sad.'

'I know,' said Fiachra.

'How many people were killed back there?'

'I don't know. I've promised Breccan I will go back with him to help bury those who died today.'

'Won't that be dangerous?'

'Well not if we make sure that the Vikings have gone first!'

'You don't think they are going to come here, do you?'

'I don't know what they will do,' said Fiachra, 'but if they come here we will be safe behind these walls.'

There was a sudden noise below them. A man was moving through the inner gates towards the Great Hall. As he walked he was staring around him, and at one point he seemed to stumble on the gravel under his feet.

'It's Dallin,' said Mor. 'He's come looking for me. I better go now or I'll be in trouble. I said I wouldn't stay out too late.'

'I'll see you again in the morning,' said Fiachra.

'Of course you will,' laughed Mor. She started to pull at the hood on her cloak; then she stopped and moved her face close to Fiachra. He stared deep into her eyes without moving. She leaned closer and kissed him. 'Goodnight, Fiachra.'

As he watched her climb down to Dallin, Fiachra thought about the day that had gone – a day full of drama and emotion. Many terrible things had happened and yet he was so happy to be here in a safe place with Mor. He thought about her kiss and he smiled to himself. Today he had fought Vikings and risked his life in battle. Yet he hadn't had the courage to kiss Mor!

The next morning dawned quickly for Fiachra as it was late when he finally found a space to lie in on the floor of the Great Hall. He would happily have spent more time resting but the hall was noisy and people were moving all around him. As he pulled himself up he looked around the room. There was no sign of Mor or Breccan but Fergus was just a few feet away from him.

'Young Fiachra! Did you sleep well?'

'Well enough – but not long enough, I'm afraid.' Fiachra looked towards the light streaming in the doorway. 'What news is there today?'

'There is no real news,' said Fergus. 'There should be more reinforcements arriving this morning from the fort at Ardifuir, according to Lochlann – although it doesn't look like we will be needing them.'

'How so?'

'There is no sign of the Norsemen,' said Fergus.

Just as he spoke, a horn rang out from the ramparts of the

fort. 'That will be the men from Ardifuir,' said Fergus. As the two men moved out of the hall into the sunlight it was clear that Fergus was right. The main gates swung open and some soldiers appeared; most were on foot, though there were some on horseback.

Fiachra felt the sun warm him as he moved down to the main enclosure. It was going to be a beautiful day. Lochlann was already down at the gates to meet the new arrivals. The leader of the soldiers dismounted and walked forward to speak to the Chief of Dunadd. 'Thank you for coming, Nem,' said Lochlann, 'but why so few men?'

'You asked for help. There are twenty four of us here,' said Nem. 'We had to leave some men to guard the dun at Ardifuir. Anyway,' he said, looking around him, 'it looks as if we are not needed.'

'What do you mean?'

'Well, where are these Norsemen?'

Fiachra went down to the main gates. He was looking for Mor but thinking about the Vikings. It was true that there was no sign of them, though there was still a small trickle of smoke visible from the hills in the east over the burned settlement at Loch Glashan. Had the Vikings contented themselves with destroying the village and stealing what they could lay their hands on? Would Ketil be willing to sail home after such a defeat?

Fiachra moved through the detachment of soldiers looking for the small group of houses. He soon saw Mor as she came out of a house with Etain.

'Good morning to you both.'

'Good morning to you, Fiachra,' said Etain.

Mor flashed a smile, 'Did you sleep well?'

'Not long enough,' said Fiachra.

Etain looked from one to the other. 'It's no wonder you are both tired. You stayed up much too late last night.'

Mor turned towards Fiachra. Her eyes were sparkling as she got ready to speak, but suddenly she stopped in her tracks. It appeared to Fiachra as if she was looking over his shoulder at someone else. As he wheeled round he saw a man step forward, leading a horse. He was big, much taller than Fiachra, with tousled brown hair and a green cloak. A sword was attached to his belt. Mor stepped forward. She spoke awkwardly.

'Fiachra, this is Conall from Ardifuir.'

'Hello,' said Fiachra as he looked up at the newcomer.

Conall towered over Fiachra, staring for a moment longer than necessary at the scar on his forehead. Then he called a greeting to Etain before turning his attention to Mor. 'I am so glad you are safe. And I'm glad I am here now to protect you.' He smiled at the girl. Then he pulled on the horse at his side. 'I have to stable my horse. I'll see you shortly. We need to talk. I hope you have been considering my proposal.' Then Conall trudged over towards the stables on the other side of the enclosure.

Fiachra turned back towards Mor. She looked worried. With Etain standing within earshot, he didn't know what to say. But as it turned out there was no chance for him to say anything. They could hear loud, animated conversation on the walls beside the gates; then a soldier cried out the words nobody wanted to hear. These words were repeated again and again throughout the fort of Dunadd as people spilled from the Great Hall, the workshops and the stables.

'The Vikings are coming!'

HILLSIDE GRAVE

It was the middle of the afternoon and the rain continued to batter against the windows of the cottage. But the children were thrilled that Dad had arrived at last and the family were together again.

Katie and Isobel had returned from their visit to the doctors. Emma decided to make a cup of tea for the grown-ups while Dad unpacked his case. A game of football was out of the question so Ben sat in the sitting room trying to set up the chess set. It was all going well until he realised he was running out of pieces to fill the board. There were two black chess pieces missing.

'What's a pawn?' asked Emma.

'Like this,' said Ben, holding up a small piece of wood for her to see. 'There are some missing. We need to find two more.'

'I think I saw two pieces like that,' said Emma.

'Where did you see them?'

'I can't remember.'

'Well, that's not much good. We can't play without all the pieces.'

Dad wandered through from the bedroom. He had changed into his slippers. For the children this was a good sign. Whenever Dad wore his slippers (which was not often), it meant he was really in holiday mood. Aunt Isobel was first to address him. 'Cameron, Emma has made some tea for you.'

'Thanks Emma,' said Dad, picking up the cup on the tray. Then he turned to his son. 'Don't worry about the two pawns. They aren't that important. We can still play. Anyway, you go white and I'll go black. That'll give you an advantage.' He sat down beside Katie on the settee, and looked over at the children. 'Okay, tell me what it is that you guys said you wanted to tell me before we begin the game.'

'We found something,' said Emma.

'Right at the top of the hill we climbed,' Ben added quickly.

'Right at the top of the hill you should *not* have climbed,' said his Dad. 'Your Mum has told me all about that incident.'

'Well okay, maybe we shouldn't have done it by ourselves,' said Emma, 'but we did anyway, and we found an old stone with writing on it, and on it is the name of two people called Fiachra and Mor.'

'They lived nine hundred years ago,' said Ben.

'How do you know that?' asked Dad.

'Colin told us,' said Emma.

'He's probably just winding you up,' said Cameron, smiling.

'Actually, Colin seems to be quite serious about it,' said

Katie, turning towards her husband. 'He wants to go up to see the stone for himself. And he says that you should come along too.'

'Well I don't mind climbing a hill, especially if the weather is okay,' said Dad, 'but I don't hold out too much hope for the stone.'

'What do you mean, hope?' asked Emma.

'Well, I don't think it's very likely to be genuine.'

'Why not?' This time it was Katie who asked the question.

'I'm not exactly an archaeologist, but writing on a stone isn't likely to have survived for nine hundred years.'

'But old gravestones...' began Emma.

'Old gravestones aren't actually all that old, Emma. And if it's meant to be a gravestone, why would it be at the top of a mountain? People get buried *underneath* mountains, not on top of them!' As Dad saw the disappointed looks on the faces of his children, he decided to change tack. 'But who knows? Maybe it will be the find of the century! If Colin is taking it seriously enough that he wants to go up that hill to take a look, then we can all do it – as long as we wait for some better weather.'

'We could wait a long time for that,' said Ben, glumly.

'Cheer up,' said Dad. 'Tonight, seeing as it's my first night, we're going out for a meal. No one here is going to cook. I thought we could go the Kilmartin Hotel. If I'm right, that will be just underneath your mountain.'

Ben was amazed. 'You want to climb the mountain tonight?'

'No!' his father laughed, patting Ben's back. 'That would be crazy. But you can show me where you went.' He stood up and moved to the table where Ben was sitting. As Cameron sat down opposite his son, he announced, 'It's time for this chess match. And I see you get all the luck.'

'What do you mean?' asked Ben.

'Well, not only do you have two extra pieces, but you're white. So that means you get to go first.' Ben smiled. He knew fine well he would need to have a lot of extra pieces before he could hope to beat his Dad.

By evening, the rain had eased off, the temperature had dropped and the sky was darker than normal. It was a bit of a struggle to persuade Isobel to join them for the meal as she rarely ate out. But in the end, they all bundled into Dad's car, with Katie squashing in beside the children in the back seat.

They drove along the road towards Kilmartin Glen – a road that was becoming very familiar to Emma and Ben – and they passed the cairns, standing stones, and the old fort of Dunadd on their way. The journey lasted only a few minutes; soon they saw the tiny village of Kilmartin looming up in front of them. To the disappointment of the children, the hills beside the village were mostly shrouded in cloud. There was nothing for them to point to.

Cameron parked the car at the old churchyard and they filed across the road to the hotel, moving more slowly than usual because Aunt Isobel was with them. She was looking around her, taking in her surroundings, when she said 'It's a long time since I was here.'

Emma was studying the building. 'Have *we* ever been here before?'

'Last time we were on holiday, your Dad and I came here to eat one evening,' said Katie, 'but this is a first for you two.

136

So make sure you behave yourselves.'

'What do you think we are going to do – start throwing food around?' asked Emma indignantly.

Ben chimed in. 'Or set fire to the place?'

'Okay, okay,' said Mum, ushering them in through the door, 'I get the picture.' Whether it was due to the fact that she wasn't cooking, or maybe because Dad had arrived at last, the children were both glad to see that their Mum was looking much more relaxed this evening.

'Look at this! Wild boar,' exclaimed Ben, as he scanned one of the long cards the waiter was passing around the table. Ben wondered if that was what people here used to eat hundreds of years ago. It certainly sounded like something a Viking might chew on.

'You won't get *that* at McDonalds,' said his father, smiling.

Emma pointed out, 'It's not on the children's menu, Ben.'

'Do we have to eat what's on the children's menu, Mum?'

Katie hesitated to answer, but Cameron leaned over to his son. 'Don't worry. I'm choosing the wild boar. I'll let you have a taste.'

The food was good though both Emma and Ben agreed that the wild boar was not as exciting as it sounded. After the meal was over and they stepped outside the hotel, they found that the midges were out in force. The tiny flies swarmed around them all as they crossed over to the car, dodging puddles on the way. 'I'd forgotten about the blasted midges,' said Cameron, as he eased the vehicle back onto the road, rubbing at his face and neck.

'You know they really haven't been too bad this year,'

said Aunt Isobel. For Cameron that was no great comfort. For some reason, the midges seemed to be particularly fond of him.

They had just settled themselves down in the cottage when there was a knock on the door. Isobel opened the door to find Colin standing there, filling the doorway. 'Pardon me for coming down so late. I noticed you were out earlier.' The big man bowed his head before stepping in to the sitting room and smiling at everyone. 'Well hello, Cameron. It's good to see you.'

The two men stood together shaking hands.

'I take it you've heard from the children about their find?' Cameron nodded. 'I said I'd like to see it for myself, and I thought we might go up Beinn Bhan. Would *you* like to come as well?'

'Of course, though I think we need to wait for a good day,' said Cameron.

'Well that's just it,' said Colin, reaching up to scratch his head. 'The forecast is actually good for tomorrow. We could go in the morning if you are all free.'

'That would be great,' said Emma, turning to her brother. Ben nodded agreement.

'What about your foot?' asked Katie.

'It's okay now, I think,' said Ben. He looked over to see his mother staring at him doubtfully. 'If it doesn't feel good in the morning I won't go,' he added.

'If its pouring in the morning, *none* of us will go,' said Cameron.

After the weather they had endured that day, it was difficult to be confident that the next day would be much better. But when the sun appeared the following morning, the air smelt fresh and clean and it was as if the rain had been used up. Katie and Isobel were staying at the cottage and they prepared a picnic for the walkers as they got ready. Soon Colin and Cameron were setting off in the car with the children in the back. Once again they were heading to Kilmartin where they had eaten the night before.

'Do you think we could become rich?' asked Emma.

'What do you mean?' replied Cameron.

'Well if this stone is something important from history, and we found it, could we get a reward?'

Keeping his hands carefully on the wheel, Dad twisted his head round to smile at her. 'Not very likely, I'm afraid!' He looked at the older man by his side. 'You don't really think this stone is genuine, do you?'

Colin shrugged. 'Who knows?'

Cameron persisted, 'But a stone with a nine hundred year old carving couldn't survive all this time.'

'Well now, Cameron, it would be quite unlikely, I'll admit. But maybe not impossible,' said Colin.

'Emma thinks it's a gravestone,' said Ben. 'It does look a bit like a gravestone.'

'Maybe Dad's right, though,' said Emma. 'Who would get buried at the top of a mountain?'

'Let's just wait and see what you have to show us,' said Cameron, as they got out of the car to begin the climb.

Ben was not sure whether his foot would be up to climbing the hill again, but he didn't want to miss out on showing the grown-ups the stone he had discovered. As they trudged upwards his foot felt fine, and with Colin and his Dad travelling beside him, the journey seemed much less risky this time. Somehow it seemed to take a lot less time, too.

When they reached the top of the hill, they stared out at the wide panorama in front of them. As they looked over to the islands in the west, everything seemed clear - just as it had the last time they had been there. The children moved into the lead, following the ridge at the trig point towards St Breccan's cell. The men were slower, as Colin kept pointing landmarks out to Cameron who had never been here before.

'What if the stone is gone?' said Ben, having a sudden attack of uncertainty. His voice was breathless from the climb.

'Don't be daft,' said Emma. 'What would be the chances of that? If the stone's been here for nine hundred years it can last another few days.'

She wanted to push him playfully on his back but she thought better of it. She'd already been blamed once for Ben falling on this hill.

When they arrived at the small pile of stones that marked the cell, the children dropped to their knees and crawled to the edge of the escarpment. There, only a few feet below them, was the torn heather and exposed earth where the stone lay. The writing was clearly visible though from this distance it was impossible to read it.

'Be careful,' said Colin, who was now hurrying to catch up, 'there's quite a drop over there.'

'We know that already,' said Emma.

'And I'm not going to forget it any time soon,' added Ben for good measure. Slowly, the four climbers worked their way down till they reached the grey slab of stone beneath them. They gazed at the wording inscribed on the rock face: 'Fiachra agus Mor'.

'It's incredible,' said Colin, squinting down and staring

closely at the slab. 'Fiachra agus Mor.' He kept repeating the words over and over as if they were some kind of chant. Cameron, concerned about the drop behind them, was keeping his eyes firmly on the children but eventually he crouched down beside Colin.

'Do you think it's real?'

'This stone is real enough,' said the older man.

'Of course it is. But are you sure it isn't a hoax?'

'What's a hoax?' asked Ben.

'A hoax is when something is false,' said Emma, proudly. Ben looked up at his Dad to see what he would say.

'What Emma says is right. It could be that someone has carved these words onto the stone recently. It might not be that old.'

'But why would someone want to do that? What would they gain?' asked Colin.

'And why would they then hide it under the heather where no one could see it?' added Emma.

Cameron traced the letters on the rock with his finger. It amazed him to feel how deeply the words were cut into the stone. He thought to himself that a carving made nearly a thousand years ago would by now have been worn away by the weather. Colin produced a camera and took a photo of the stone. Cameron did the same with his phone.

'So what do we do now?' asked Emma.

Dad looked over to his children. 'I don't really know whether this is a serious discovery or not, but you've done well to find it, and I think we should speak to someone. But I don't know who that would be.'

Colin stood up and stretched himself. 'I think we should speak to Sheila Campbell.'

'Who's that?' asked Emma.

'She's the Curator at the Kilmartin House Museum.'

He saw the blank expressions on the faces of Ben and Emma. 'That means she's the boss,' explained Colin. 'She ought to be able to help us.'

'What *is* this place anyway?' Cameron asked Colin, after they had climbed back up to Breccan's Cell. He was leaning against one of the stones that jutted skywards from the grassy ridge, looking for the sandwiches and crisps in his rucksack.

'Well, Breccan seems to be a real historical person. He was a priest who was active in this area nine hundred years ago. He was apparently much loved and he organised the building of some churches in the area. This was a quiet place that he used to come to on retreat. He came up here to pray and find solitude.'

'And to get a brilliant view,' suggested Emma.

'That's true, Emma,' laughed Colin. 'It's certainly a great view!'

Cameron was deep in thought. 'nine hundred years ago…. I've heard that before,' he said.

Colin nodded. 'That's right. Breccan was living around these parts at the same time as Fiachra and Mor. He was well known to them both.'

'Don't you think it's interesting that a stone with names from nine hundred years ago should be found here at a site connected to another person who lived nine hundred years ago?'

'I think it's very interesting indeed,' said Colin. 'We need to go down to see Ms Campbell. If this stone turns out to be important, it's amazing how close it is to her museum.'

After sharing lunch at the top of Beinn Bhan, the four carefully descended the hill and walked along the path beside the road which wound back to the village of Kilmartin. At the centre, across from the hotel and next to the church, stood the entrance gates to the museum grounds. 'Let's hope it's open today,' said Ben to Emma, as they walked to the reception door.

At the front desk, Emma was given the honour of speaking. 'We would like to talk to Ms Campbell,' she said. The woman behind the till was pleasant but firm.

'I'm sorry, but she is very busy today.'

Colin intervened. 'Listen, could you tell her it's Colin from Achnabreck. We just want a wee minute of her time. I promise it won't take long.'

The words seemed to do the trick. 'Colin, I didn't see you there,' said the woman. 'Just take a seat in the café and I'll call her.'

Ben was looking around the place. 'Where is she, anyway?'

'She works in the house next door,' said Colin. 'It used to be the church manse but now it's part of the museum.'

Cameron bought some juice for them all and they sat down at a table. One of the walls beside them consisted of a continuous sheet of glass – like a giant window with views down the glen. Dotted around the landscape were piles of stones; the remains of ancient burial places.

A woman appeared beside their table. She wore a jumper over a long flowing dress. Though her dark hair was short and neat, to Ben and Emma she looked like a hippie and much younger than they would have imagined someone who was in charge of a museum to be. 'Hello,' she said cheerily.

'My name is Sheila Campbell. And I know *you*, Colin.'

As she sat down at the table, Colin introduced her to everybody. 'The children here have found something that is very interesting – a stone with an inscription on it. I'll let them tell you the story themselves.'

Ben and Emma related the tale of climbing Beinn Bhan and how they came to find the carved rock. Sheila listened intently until they had finished. But then, instead of speaking, everything went quiet. She seemed lost in thought. Colin broke the silence. 'Sheila, have you ever heard the old stories of Fiachra and Mor? I was told them when I was small.'

'I have heard of them,' she said. 'I come from Edinburgh, so I wasn't brought up in this part of Scotland, but since I've been living and working here I've tried to read as much as I can about the area.'

'You mean the stories are actually in print?' asked Colin, in surprise.

'Yes, I'm sure I read of them in some book on old Scottish folk tales. But I always thought they were just in myths and legends, not real historical people.'

'Could they be real?' asked Emma.

'I'll need to go up and see for myself,' said Sheila. 'When I see this stone I'll probably have a good idea. If there is a chance that this a stone from the 12th Century, I'll need to call in some real experts to take a look.' Then she stood up from the table. 'It was good to meet you all but I need to go now. When I get a chance to check this stone, I'll give you a phone, Colin.'

As Dad drove the car homeward, Colin shouted behind him, 'You kids should be archaeologists when you grow up!'

'We don't even know that the stone is real yet,' said Ben.

'That's true, but you've got the curator of Kilmartin Museum agreeing to climb that hill just to check on your story. So it means she is taking you seriously. And it means there is a chance that you have made a very important discovery.' The children sat in the back feeling quite pleased with themselves. Cameron asked, 'What do you two want to do this evening?'

'Swimming baths!' shouted Emma.

'Don't be daft. The pool will be shut,' said Ben. 'Football!'

Emma sighed. 'Not football! Anyway, what about your foot?'

'We've not played football all holiday,' protested Ben. 'My foot is okay. You can go in goal.'

Emma didn't like the sound of that. 'What about the midges?'

'Let's just wait and see,' said Dad.

THE CHALLENGE

Instinctively, Fiachra started moving towards the outer walls of the fort. He found himself at a small stairway leading up to the ramparts. Others had the same idea and a small queue began forming at the bottom of the stairs. Before Fiachra was able to make his way up to the ledge where the shouts had been heard, another cry rang out. There was a company of people approaching Dunadd from the north, and although they had only just come into view, they were advancing fast.

Looking over the walls, Fiachra could see a large group of Norsemen heading across the bog directly ahead of him. They were following the route that the Gaels had taken the evening before. As he turned to his left, he could see a much smaller but closer band of about twenty people heading through the Kilmartin Glen. Two men led the way on horseback, though most of the others were on foot. The sunlight reflected on spears and helmets.

146

Fiachra turned to the soldier beside him. 'Who are these people?' The soldier shrugged his shoulders. It was still hard to tell from this distance. From along the wall Gabran's voice was clearly heard calling down to Lochlann.

'It looks as if there could be at least two hundred men,' he said to his chief.

'Vikings!' cried another voice. 'These are more Vikings approaching from the north!' Heads turned to stare at the smaller band of people. As they drew nearer, it was possible to make out the differences in their clothing. The men wore tunics with high collars and looked more like Fiachra than the others in the castle.

Fiachra knew that the main group of Vikings heading towards him would be Ketil and warriors from the ships he had already seen arriving at Asknish, but the presence of the other group was a mystery. Then a sentry was heard shouting, 'It's Kjartan!' This meant nothing to Fiachra. He was aware that Cathal was now standing beside him on the ledge. He turned to the leather worker for an explanation.

'Kjartan is a Viking,' he said. 'He lives some miles north of here with his relatives. But he has always lived peacefully with us. Until now.'

Kjartan and his followers approached Dunadd directly, as if they were set to enter the fort, but on Lochlann's orders the main gate remained closed and barred. From the top of the walls, Gabran shouted down at the newcomers. 'What is your business here?' Kjartan reined in his horse and looked up at the people on the battlements.

'We have come to offer you our assistance. There are not many of us, but we will do what we can to help you.' Lochlann began to climb up to the rampart himself as

147

Fiachra looked down at the mounted Viking and his men. Kjartan was a handsome man with a beard and hair that appeared pale yellow in the sunlight. A rich, blue cloak hung from his shoulders, yet his helmet appeared only to be made of leather.

Gabran was in conversation with Lochlann. 'We cannot open the gate to them. It's a trap. Once they come in, they will attack us.'

Lochlann put one hand on his friend's shoulder and, with the other, pointed outwards to the larger company of men crossing the bog. 'These men are not at our gates yet,' he said. 'We have little to fear. If we let Kjartan in now, and he tries to attack us, we will soon kill him and everyone who is with him.'

In a loud voice, Lochlann announced, 'Open the gates!' To the dismay of many of the defenders, the gates swung open and Kjartan entered with his men. He dropped from his horse and walked over to Lochlann who was descending the stairs. For a moment, the attention of the watchers shifted to what was happening inside the enclosure.

'Why have you come here?' asked the chief.

'We have come to offer our help.'

'You would fight your own people?' asked Lochlann, with some surprise.

'I hope there will be no need to fight,' said Kjartan, 'but I live here now and I seek peace. There will be no peace if villages are burned and people massacred by pirates like Ketil the Cruel.'

'It seems as if your pirate has found some extra friends,' said Lochlann. 'There have been many sightings of longships over these last days.'

'I can tell you more news,' said Kjartan. 'The King is dead.'

Lochlann's mouth dropped open. 'King Edgar is dead?'

'No, King Magnus. He was killed in Ireland and what remains of his army is now returning to Norway.'

'That explains the sightings of these ships,' said Gabran, as the news spread throughout the crowd.

'But now we have this place to defend,' said Lochlann, regaining composure. Then he beckoned to someone standing behind him. Breccan strode forward to the centre of the enclosure. He lifted his hands above him, and, at the signal, everyone knelt on the ground to pray. 'Great God, and Father of us all,' he began, 'protect us today from our enemies. May this place be a safe refuge for us. May you guard us and guide us as we face this test. And may your peace preserve our land. Amen.'

As the people rose to their feet, Gabran's voice called out: 'Get the archers to the walls!' As people began rushing around in all directions, Fiachra became aware that Kjartan was first staring at him and then, walking towards him.

'Who are you?' asked the Norseman.

'My name is Fiachra. I come from Ederline.'

'Ederline is near to where I live now.'

Fiachra realised that Kjartan was confused by his appearance. He looked down at his clothes as he spoke. 'Three years ago I was kidnapped by Ketil and taken to his home in the north. I have only just made my escape.'

'No doubt Ketil is looking for you.'

Fiachra nodded. 'No doubt,' he said.

As Kjartan climbed up the wall, Fiachra went looking for Mor. This time Etain was nowhere to be seen and he spotted the girl standing on her own. As Fiachra approached he could see the furrow on her brow and concern in her eyes. 'Don't worry, Mor. Those Vikings can't get in here. Breccan is right. God will protect us here.' Mor didn't speak, but her eyes met his. She looked so vulnerable.

'I must go now and help at the wall. I'll see if I can get a bow and stand with the archers.' Before he moved away from Mor he put his arms around her shoulders and hugged her close. 'Be careful,' said Mor, as he reluctantly pulled away. Once again he had the feeling that he was being watched. He could see Kjartan ahead of him but he had his back to Fiachra. As he moved up the stairway, Fiachra saw Conall with a group of men near the gate. Conall was staring at him coldly, with anger in his eyes.

Looking out from the wall towards The Moss once more, Fiachra was surprised at how near the Vikings were to the fort. They had halted their march and were fanning out in a broad line. Near the centre of the group Fiachra recognised Ketil and Gris. They were standing next to a man dressed in chainmail who seemed to be one of the leaders. From the behaviour of the men it appeared that they were having some kind of argument.

Fergus was now at Fiachra's shoulder. 'These black-hearted butchers are in trouble now,' he said.

'What do you mean?'

'Well they have caught up with us, but they didn't know about this place. These walls will keep them out. They can burn our homes and workshops on the island but they can never defeat us – as long as we stay here.'

'I hope you are right, Fergus,' said Fiachra. 'But suppose they just stay there and try to starve us out?'

'How long would that take? They won't have the patience,' said Fergus confidently.

'I know Ketil well,' said Fiachra. 'He won't give up easily. And if he does leave, you can be sure he will be back.'

The Vikings stood in position as if ready to charge but there was no signal to attack. All of the defenders were inside the Dunadd fort, safe for the time being.

'I'm going down to see if someone will give me a bow, and then I'll join the archers,' said Fiachra to Fergus. He started along the walkway towards the top of the stairs but as he neared the stairway, a big figure was blocking his path. It was Conall. And he didn't look happy.

'Keep away from Mor,' he barked. 'She belongs to me.'

'I didn't know she belonged to anyone,' said Fiachra, as calmly as he could.

By now the two men were facing each other. Conall stood over Fiachra, glowering down at him. 'Mor and I will be married soon.'

'I'm not sure that Mor agrees with that,' said Fiachra.

Conall's hand reached up to Fiachra's throat. 'Just stay away,' he repeated. His eyes darted around, as he made sure that no one else was listening. They were surrounded by people and Conall knew that he dare not start a fight at a time like this.

By the time Fiachra had helped himself to a bow and returned to the wall, the Vikings were on the move. One of them started walking slowly and deliberately towards the fortress. As he drew near to the gates he stopped. Fiachra didn't recognise him as one of Ketil's crew. He was a small man, and the axe and shield he carried seemed too big for him. But his voice was loud and clear. 'We seek no battle here.' The words were unexpected. 'We are heading home to the north. We ask only one thing. Surrender Fiachra to us, and we will be on our way.'

Despite his advancing years, Lochlann's reply was equally strong and firm. 'You ask only one thing?' he repeated. 'When you have butchered our people and destroyed our homes?' As he said this, he raised his arm in the direction of Loch Glashan. 'We owe you nothing. So go now, and never return here again.'

The small Viking made no reply but turned on his heels and began trudging back to his comrades.

Fiachra was aware that people around him were talking about him – not everyone in Dunadd knew his story and why he should be wanted so badly by the Vikings. As he looked around, he could see groups of people conferring. Down below were a few of the armed men from Ardifuir. He saw Conall in that group. He couldn't hear what he was saying but every few moments he saw the big man turn and look up his way.

Suddenly, Mor was at his side. 'Are you alright, Fiachra? I heard what the Viking said. Don't worry, we will never give you up. We are all safe here.' Fiachra smiled down at her. It was her turn to try and comfort him. 'Etain has made some food and she has invited you to join us. Come and eat now.'

Fiachra took a last look at the Vikings before following Mor to the stairs. The messenger had returned with the reply from Dunadd. Ketil could be seen stomping about, throwing his arms in the air. The man with the suit of chainmail was still beside him, hardly moving at all.

Fiachra sat on the grass with Etain, Dallin and Mor. In front of him was stew in a wooden bowl; he was grateful for

152

the food and the chance to rest his legs. Overhead the sky was bright and cloudless. It was a beautiful and peaceful day, the silence above only broken by the occasional sound of circling gulls – a huge contrast to the tension everyone was feeling inside the settlement of Dunadd. But the lull was short; a shout from the walls alerted everyone that the Viking messenger was once again making his way to the main gates of the fort.

Fiachra climbed back on to the wall, and watched the Norseman approach. This time there was no axe or shield. Instead he carried a long spear. When he arrived at the spot where he had spoken before, he thrust the spear deep into the ground before making his new announcement. 'Lord Ketil wants to speak with you. Five of your men must come here to meet five of ours. Everyone else must keep their distance.' Before waiting for a reply, the Viking turned away from Dunadd and began walking back towards Ketil.

A quiet fell over the people in the fort as they looked towards Lochlann to see what he would say. He bowed his head and was silent for a few minutes. 'It could be a trap. We don't need to do anything,' said Gabran.

But Lochlann looked over at the people in front of him and said quietly but firmly, 'We should hear what they want to say.'

'*You* must not go there. Let me go instead,' said Gabran.

'Very well,' replied the chieftain, 'take Nem with you ... and Conaing from the loch ... and your friend Tuathal ... and take Kjartan too. You may need him to speak to these Vikings.'

He looked up to the wall. 'Archers! Make sure your weapons are ready. Open fire at the first sign of treachery!'

The soldiers at the gate raised the bar and pushed the doors open and the five men walked towards the spear that stood as a marker in the marsh. Tuathal was a powerfully built soldier from Dunadd. He was the only one of the group that Fiachra did not know.

Seeing the men emerge from the walls, five of the Vikings now started out towards the spear. Fiachra recognised only Ketil and Gris, though the chief in chainmail was walking alongside the others. Voices were lowered as they began to talk and it was impossible to hear what was being said. The meeting went on for a long time.

Fiachra felt a movement by his side and Mor was there with him. She linked her arm in his as they both watched from the wall. The wind blew her dark hair across her face and she kept having to push it away with her hand. A soldier drew near to her, 'You shouldn't be up here,' he said. 'it's too dangerous on this wall.' But there was no time to reply. The conversation on The Moss had ended; the five men were now returning to the fort.

Once they were safely inside and the gates fastened behind them, Lochlann announced a meeting in the Great Hall. Leaving sentries patrolling the battlements, everyone moved up to the biggest building of Dunadd. Sitting in his customary seat, Lochlann motioned for Gabran to speak. The hall was overflowing with people with many more looking in from outside. Fiachra and Mor were inside near the back of the building.

'The Vikings have offered an arrangement,' Gabran began. 'One of them is Ketil. It was he who attacked the village of Asknish and he has raided our shores many times before. There is another leader called Ragnar who has come

154

here from fighting with King Magnus. They are on their way back to Norway and are tired of war. They see that our defences are strong, and that to lay siege to this place would take a long time. They do not want to do it.'

'Well, let them go then!' shouted someone in the crowd. It seemed an obvious thing to say and others murmured their approval.

'Wait a moment,' continued Gabran. 'I'm not finished. Ketil says he cannot leave until he has avenged his honour. His son was killed by Fiachra and he demands payment.'

Now there was unrest throughout the crowd. It seemed as if all eyes had turned to stare at Fiachra. Someone else shouted out, 'What payment can we make?'

Gabran continued. 'He says that he must fight Fiachra to gain justice for his family. Win or lose, when the fight is over, the Vikings swear that they will leave this place.'

'What if we refuse?' asked Lochlann.

'Then they will stay here and besiege the castle.'

Fiachra's head swam. Colour drained from his face and he was aware of his heart beating wildly. His legs felt unsteady. At the same time, he could feel Mor's fingers on his arm gripping him tightly.

Kjartan stood up. 'There is no justice in a seasoned warrior like Ketil fighting a young boy. What chance would Fiachra stand against him? We must refuse this request. Most of the Vikings out there are under the control of Ragnar. I know something of Ragnar; I know that he is keen to return north and that he wants Ketil to go with him. He will not be persuaded to stay and lay siege to this place. Without Ragnar and his men, Ketil could never defeat us.'

The noise in the Great Hall increased as the people began

to talk among themselves, until someone shouted out above the crowd, 'What if you are wrong? If we refuse the Vikings, we may all die at their hands. Accepting their offer is better than taking that risk.'

'We cannot send someone to their death,' said Fergus, standing beside Conaing, who was nodding agreement as he spoke. 'Fiachra fought with us on the loch and he has done all he can to help us.'

'But we aren't doing that!' The speaker was a tall man near the back of the hall, on the other side from Fiachra and Mor. He wore a long green cloak and he was walking forward as he spoke. 'We aren't sending anyone to their death,' continued Conall. 'This is a duel – one against one. Who knows who will win? If God is on our side, will God not see that justice is done and protect this Fiachra – even though he has clearly brought this trouble our way? If the Vikings are prepared to leave us in peace after the duel, then I say this offer is a good one. Why should we risk our lives and the future of this place by turning them down and risking a war?'

Conall looked over towards Fiachra, and saw, to his disgust, that Mor was standing by his side. He went on, again. 'We have just heard that Fiachra fought at the battle on the loch, so clearly he is old enough to fight. Why cannot he fight now? Perhaps because he is a coward and would rather save his own skin than the lives of the people around him.'

There was a gasp from the listeners at this insult. To Fiachra, it felt like a stinging slap on the face. A man had been pushing his way through the crowd and now he broke through to where Fiachra was standing. He threw a protective arm over the young man. 'Do not listen to these words. You will not have to fight Ketil. We will not let that happen.'

Fiachra looked into the kindly eyes of Breccan but even as he did so, he was aware of something stirring within him. It was like that day at the loch when he had suddenly felt he must risk everything – including his own life – to protect the people around him. He didn't know what it was that he was hearing; he only knew that he had to listen to that voice.

Despite waves of fear surging over him at the prospect of meeting Ketil, he gently pushed his friend's hands away as he stepped forward. And he heard his voice clearly – though it seemed almost as if someone else was speaking, 'I will do it. I will fight Ketil.'

Shouting broke out in the hall as Lochlann vainly appealed for calm. Mor flung herself on Fiachra, pulling at him as if she were trying to take him away. 'Fiachra! No! No! You must not do this!' she screamed.

Across from them, Conall stood quite still, watching the scene. There was a broad smile on his face.

LEGBITER'S RETURN

A small chapel stood behind the Great Hall, and Fiachra sat there with Breccan at his side. It was cool and dark despite the brightness of the day outside. Calm was gradually being restored. They were apart from the crowds at last; Etain and Dallin had managed to prise Mor away from Fiachra as she continued to cry and shout at the young man to change his mind.

A shadow appeared at the doorway and Kjartan asked Breccan's permission to enter. The monk beckoned him inside. The Norseman crouched down beside Fiachra. The young man was sitting motionless, staring into space.

'I don't really know you at all,' Kjartan said. 'I can see that you are brave. But you don't need to fight this man. He has killed so many people. If you refuse to fight him, he will have no choice but to leave. Ragnar wants to go home; if he goes, he will take his men with him.'

'How can we trust what Ragnar says? How can we trust Vikings?'

Kjartan said softly, 'I am a Viking. We are not all like Ketil.'

Fiachra turned towards him. 'I am sorry,' he said, 'forgive me. I did not mean to offend you.'

'Don't you see?' said Kjartan. 'You don't need to fight. Ketil will have to leave here.'

'He may leave, but then he will come back. I'll never be free of him. Sooner or later I will have to face Ketil. He will not give up.' Fiachra turned to the Viking beside him and grasped his arm. 'Thank you for trying to help me,' he said.

Fiachra sat alone with his friend in the quiet of the chapel. Breccan had asked that Fiachra be given time on his own. 'Lochlann has sent the Norsemen a message. The combat will take place in the morning,' said the priest.

'Will God help me tomorrow?'

'Of course he will,' answered Breccan.

'How will he do that?' asked Fiachra.

'Well, I think God honours those who honour God,' said the monk.

'Am I honouring God?'

'You are putting your own life in danger in order to save others. I believe God will honour that.'

'So, can I win?'

There was a silence. 'It is possible,' said the priest, realising immediately that his words didn't sound convincing. 'Remember that David defeated the giant Goliath. It *is* possible,' Breccan repeated, trying this time to sound more confident.

'Can I stay here?' asked Fiachra. 'Can I sleep in here tonight?'

'Of course you can,' said Breccan, standing to leave. 'I'll see to it that you are not disturbed.'

It was nearly an hour later when Breccan returned. 'There are lots of people asking for you and wanting to speak to you – including Lochlann. But I've told them you want some peace for now.'

'Thank you,' said Fiachra.

'But there is someone here who I thought you might want to speak to now.'

'Who is it?'

'It's Mor,' replied Breccan.

At the sound of her name, the girl entered the chapel and sat down next to Fiachra. Her eyes were wet with tears but she had stopped crying. 'Why have you agreed to this, Fiachra? After all this time when I thought I would never see you again? Now you have come back at last and you choose to fight this evil man? How can you do this?'

'Mor, listen to this. Ketil is after me. He wants my blood. He will not rest. If I don't do this, then I will always be on the run. Ketil will never give up. It's a way of keeping you safe – and all the other people here. If I should fall tomorrow, at least no others will lose their lives.'

Fiachra reached out for her hand. His mind was filled with the encounter with Ketil but somehow he could hardly bear to speak of it with Mor. So he tried to think of a way to speak of other things. 'I don't think much of your boyfriend.'

Mor sat up indignantly. 'Conall is not my boyfriend,' she said.

'I'm glad to hear it. Because you deserve so much better.'

'I'll never marry him. If I ever marry anyone it will be you.'

The words burned themselves into Fiachra's mind. They stayed with him as he continued to speak with Mor and after she left him. And he heard them again and again as he laid himself down to sleep in the chapel that night. *If I ever marry anyone it will be you.*

Breccan lay across from him, still and quiet, on a thin mat on the floor of the chapel. He had promised to pray for Fiachra. Looking over towards him in the darkness, it was not possible to know if he was still awake.

Fiachra's body also lay still, but his mind was spinning around in circles as he thought over and over again about the decision he had made. Was he mad? Questions filled his head, relentlessly.

What chance did he have in a fight with Ketil? Why hadn't he listened to Breccan and Mor and Kjartan, and those from the loch who had tried to stand up for him? Had he just been tricked into this foolishness by Conall?

And what about the words of Mor? Was she serious about marrying him, or was she saying that to try to give him comfort? What about God? Was God real? Would God protect him?

Fiachra sat bolt upright. Pulling out the sword Conaing had given him, he examined it. He read again the word INGELRII etched onto the surface of the blade. There was no doubt that it was a good sword. As he lay it down beside him he thought of Ketil. He had a good sword too.

The morning was dull and grey; rain seemed to be not far away. As Fiachra fastened his sword and stepped out of the chapel there was no sign of the heaving crowd in the Great Hall. Instead, he could see that people were scattered throughout the fort. As he moved towards the house where Mor was staying, he was aware that all eyes were following him.

161

Lochlann was standing at the inner gates waiting for him to pass. 'We are all grateful for what you are doing, Fiachra. You are saving many lives by this action today. And by God's grace, may you save your own.'

'Thank you,' said Fiachra. He grasped Lochlann's arm for a moment before continuing his journey.

Mor was waiting for him near the outer wall. Etain and Dallin stood beside her. Part of Fiachra wanted to be with Mor alone; yet, part of him didn't know what he could say. But as he drew near she came up to him and threw her arms around his shoulders. They stood together in silence.

The moment of quiet was broken by the sound of men walking towards them from the main gate. Fergus, Cathal and Conaing were heading towards Fiachra, with Kjartan close on their heels. Their expressions were black. 'Ketil has been looking for you already,' said Conaing. 'He's been shouting for us to open the gates, and trying to make out that you are a coward. At least that's what Kjartan tells us he has been saying.'

Kjartan caught up with the group. 'It's true. I think Ketil has not enjoyed his night in The Moss, and Ragnar is anxious to be on his way.'

'Well, I must go out and meet him then,' said Fiachra. He leaned over Mor once more, kissed her forehead, then turned and started towards the outer gates. Dallin and Etain held Mor back to stop her from running after him. As he walked, Fiachra wanted to turn round to her but he knew he couldn't bear to see her distress. Once he reached the wall, the soldiers unbarred the gates.

He heard a voice by his side. 'You are not going out alone.' It was Fergus. Cathal and Kjartan were with him,

162

along with four archers who had come down from the wall. 'We are coming with you.' As the gates opened, Fiachra heard his name being called. Breccan was running towards him.

They embraced. 'God be with you,' the monk whispered into his friend's ear.

Then they were outside the walls of Dunadd, descending the slope and heading for the spear that still stood where it had been rammed into the ground, its shaft pointing to the heavens. 'You'd better wait here,' said Fiachra, knowing that his companions couldn't come any closer to the fighting than the Vikings themselves. He was sweating already as he drew his sword.

The familiar figure of Ketil approached him. There was pure hatred in his glare. 'You have betrayed us, after all we have done for you. Now you will die!'

'After all you have done for me?' said Fiachra, in amazement. 'You killed my father and took me as your slave for three years!'

'Today I am going to avenge the death of my son Runolf.' Ketil paused, and to Fiachra's surprise, carelessly threw the sword he was carrying onto the ground. 'But I don't need *this*!'

He began to walk back to the Viking lines where someone was already heading towards him. It was the chieftain Ragnar, the one with the coat of mail. In his hands he was carrying what looked like a sword in its scabbard; he was holding it reverently, as if it were a religious object.

As Ketil pulled the sword free, the ivory shining from the handgrip, Fiachra knew he had seen it somewhere before. Ketil was about to remind him anyway. 'This is Legbiter, the sword of King Magnus. With this sword the King killed many men. Today I will use it to kill one more!'

The group behind Fiachra were watching the Vikings with suspicion. Kjartan shouted over to Ketil. 'You have given your word that you will leave after this fight?'

'I have given my word; Ragnar has given his word; we have all given our word,' said Ketil. 'Win or lose, we will leave you after this.' He paced back and forth, flexing his arm, getting used to the feel and the weight of the sword which was in his grasp.

Then with a loud cry, Ketil threw himself at Fiachra. Legbiter whistled through the air as the Viking came straight towards the boy, swinging the weapon in wide arcs nearer and nearer to his head. The onlookers heard the sound of crashing steel as Fiachra lifted his sword to parry the blows. He knew how to defend himself but his opponent was much stronger than he was. He found himself being forced backwards into the bog, stumbling under the force of Ketil's lunges, and almost losing his footing.

Most of the Great Moss surrounding Dunadd was a barren and open landscape. There were only a few trees around them, but as Fiachra continued to be forced back he found himself crashing against solid bark, unable to retreat further.

To his right was the fortress; on the wall he was aware of a blur of faces. Somewhere in that crowd were Breccan and Mor and he was desperate to see them again. But now he was struggling for breath, winded from crashing into the trunk. He watched to see what Ketil would do next.

Fiachra had heard stories of this famous sword and how it had got its name. A favourite tactic of King Magnus was to attack people by slicing low at their legs. Once he had felled them, it was a simple matter to finish them off. But Ketil was aiming high. The sword sliced through the air towards his neck. Instinctively Fiachra threw himself down to the ground and the sword buried itself in the tree. For a second Ketil was unguarded as he struggled to free Legbiter from the wood, but it was all Fiachra could do to crawl away from the Viking and try to get back onto his feet.

By the time Fiachra was standing and ready to fight, Ketil was upon him once more. Again, Fiachra found himself pushed backwards, the sword's relentless blows raining down on him. The truth was dawning on him. He was managing to counter the efforts of Ketil but it was only a matter of time before the Viking's superior strength would tell. He could never defeat the older warrior by being defensive.

Now Fiachra took the initiative as Ketil paused for breath; he moved towards the bigger man, swinging his sword in front of him. For the first time, Ketil found himself forced backwards, and having to counter the swings of Fiachra. But his discomfort did not last long, and to Fiachra's frustration, he started to laugh out loud at his young opponent. 'You are no match for a Viking! You are not even a man!'

It was then that Fiachra fell over. Stooping low to block a cut aimed at his legs, he parried the blow, but lost his balance. As Fiachra struggled to regain his footing, Legbiter swung again towards his neck. Had it landed, the contest would have been over. Such a blow would have severed his head from his body. Fiachra ducked. The blade missed his neck but glanced off the top of his head.

The force of the impact knocked him over onto his back. He felt dizzy, but he knew he had been lucky. As he looked towards his opponent, he felt something running into his eyes, blinding him. He wiped his forehead and saw that his hands showed red. Blood was flooding into his eyes from the gash above them.

Fiachra could hear the sound of cheering from the Vikings as they saw his distress. Ketil stood smiling down at him. He was enjoying this day and he was happy to extend the moment before killing the young man lying at his feet. As Fiachra struggled to get up, he found he was groggy and light-headed. He tried moving his head but that only caused more blood to run into his eyes and distort his vision.

Ahead of him stood Ketil; behind him stood his companions. He could see from their faces that that they believed the fight was nearly over. As he fought to plant his feet firmly on the ground beneath him and force himself to his feet, Ketil moved in for the kill, grinning at him horribly. Again, Fiachra began to contemplate his own death. He could only hope that if he died today, others would be spared.

Some words floated into his head:

Remember that David defeated the giant Goliath.

If I ever marry anyone it will be you.

Remember that David defeated the giant Goliath.

If I ever marry anyone it will be you...

He pitched himself forward, thinking of Mor, thinking of Breccan and knowing that this was his only chance. As the two fighters exchanged strokes he put all his strength and effort into each one, knowing that he would soon tire, but hoping to take Ketil by surprise. For a while he staggered on in blind fury. For the first time, fear appeared in the Viking's eyes.

The two swords went on crashing together with massive force; for once Ketil began to slip. Fiachra jabbed his sword at the Viking's head. Ketil narrowly avoided the blow. The next clash of blades ended in disaster. Fiachra heard the harsh rasp of metal, and when the two men pulled away, he could see that his sword's blade had been shattered. The weapon was useless.

Another cheer was heard from the Vikings as Ketil strode forward, the smile back on his face. Fiachra dropped his useless sword and began to walk backwards as Ketil closed in on him, Legbiter still intact and gleaming in his hands. One blow from the sword would kill Fiachra, but Ketil wanted to prolong his moment of triumph a little longer. He marched forward and placed a kick firmly on his opponent's stomach.

Fiachra felt his legs buckling beneath him. He crashed down onto his back as Ketil moved ever nearer. Now the Viking was holding the sword with two hands, preparing to drive it through Fiachra's fallen body and into the ground beneath. Fiachra knew the duel was ending as the big man above him moved in for the kill.

It was as he lay there panting for breath, his body tensing in anticipation of the lethal thrust, that he noticed a strange sight. At first he thought he was dreaming. His head swam, and his eyes were straining to see through the blood still flowing from the wound in his head. Now, in this altered state, he wondered if those eyes were playing tricks.

Lying in the ground beside him was a sword, almost completely hidden in the undergrowth. His mind was racing wildly. *There was no reason for a sword to be there. There was no chance that a sword could be there.* Then he remembered that Ketil had thrown his own sword on the ground before the fight. And he knew what he had to do.

As Ketil leaned over him brandishing the king's weapon, Fiachra suddenly twisted himself round, clawing for the sword at his side and quickly bringing it up towards the Viking in one motion. The sword connected clumsily with Ketil's hip, and his body buckled over with the impact.

With his last reserve of energy, the younger man struggled to his feet, and looked at the Norseman. The injury was not serious, but it had taken Ketil by surprise and he clutched at the wound in his leg, looking down to inspect the damage. Fiachra knew he had only one chance to strike before his opponent straightened up. He threw himself at Ketil, thrusting the blade towards his neck. His arm shuddered as the sword made contact with bone and Fiachra found himself locked together with the older man.

For a moment time seemed to freeze. Ketil's mouth opened, but no sound was heard. Slowly his body began to crumple, his legs gave way and he folded onto the ground beneath him. Ketil was dead.

Fiachra dropped to his knees, his energy spent. As Fergus moved forward to help him to his feet, only Ragnar moved towards the lifeless body of Ketil. Cathal and Kjartan walked forward to join him. 'Thank you for keeping your word,' said Kjartan.

'I just want to go home,' said Ragnar. 'But there is something I need to get here.' He picked up the legendary sword and knelt down to clean the blood off the blade.

Kjartan asked, 'Will you keep the sword for yourself?'

Ragnar laughed bitterly. 'This is Legbiter – the King's own sword. No one else should have it. It would bring them bad luck.'

He gazed down at the lifeless body of Ketil as if to make his point. 'I will take it back to my country where it belongs.' Then he turned and walked away.

FAREWELL TO
THE MIDGES

There was a jeep moving up the hill to the Achnabreck cottages. Emma noticed it first as she was standing near the kitchen window. 'It's not one of the usual forestry lorries,' said Aunt Isobel, 'though it looks a wee bit familiar.' The jeep slowed down as it neared the cottages and halted at the end of Isobel's driveway.

'I think it's Sheila Campbell from the museum,' said Isobel to Emma. Sure enough, Sheila emerged from the vehicle, though not before sounding the horn loudly. As Emma came down the path to meet her, Sheila explained the meaning of her action.

'Hello, Emma, I'm just letting Colin know that I am here.'

Emma smiled back at her. 'I'm sure you've let Dad and Ben know too. They're playing football in the back garden.'

As the two footballers came round the side of the cottage,

Emma's mother emerged from inside and introduced herself. 'I'm Katie,' she said, shaking Sheila's hand.

'Come away in,' said Isobel. 'We'll get the kettle on, and I'm sure Colin will be down in a minute.'

As they sat down in the main room, Emma noticed the redness of the faces of both Ben and her Dad. It amazed her that even on holiday boys had to take their football so seriously! Sheila hung her Barbour jacket on a peg behind the door. Underneath the heavy outdoor coat she was wearing a thin jumper and jeans.

Colin arrived with perfect timing – just as the tea was being poured. 'Now that you are here, Colin, I'll explain the reason for my visit,' began Sheila. 'Yesterday I climbed Beinn Bhan to take a look at your find. I took Brian with me. He works at the museum too. We took a look at your stone.'

'Did you find it okay?' asked Ben.

'Yes,' laughed Sheila, 'you gave me clear instructions. It was easy to find.'

'And what did you make of it? Is it just a fake?' asked Emma, fearing the worst.

'Well that's just it,' replied Sheila. 'The thing is, we don't quite know what to make of it."

Emma made one of her frowns. 'What do you mean?'

'Well, the interesting thing is that it appears to us to look totally genuine. The stone is not native to the hill – in fact it's similar to the stones that were used to make St Breccan's cell. Those were carried up to the top of the hill and set in place around nine hundred years ago.'

'So the children have discovered something important?' suggested Colin.

'You may have, indeed,' said Sheila, looking from Emma

to Ben. 'The only problem is that we don't understand it. You see, the carving looks to be old, and we discovered some decorative patterns etched onto the side of the slab that are similar to the ones in the old chapel of St Bride at Asknish, which may have been built around the same time.'

'Well, what don't you understand?' asked Colin.

'It's just that it's all so unusual. Not only is it strange that the carving on the stone is so well preserved after all these years, it's very hard to work out what the stone is meant to be. It's not normal to have writing on a nine hundred-year old stone in the first place. We'll check to see if there are bodies buried up there but it's an unlikely place for a grave.'

Ben leaned forward in his seat. 'Are you going to go back there again?'

'We probably will, Ben, but the next stage is to get some other people to check it out.'

'Like…?'

'Like the Carved Stones Panel. They're the experts. And they're coming out to have a look at this.'

'Is there really a Carved Stones Panel?' asked Cameron.

'Believe it or not,' laughed Sheila, getting to her feet.

'If they agree that it is a genuine carving, then we have got something very exciting on our hands. And a story that was once thought of as no more than legend turns out to be true after all.' She looked down at the children, as she made ready to leave. 'Well done, both of you. I'll let you know as soon as the panel have had a chance to come and examine your stone.'

Emma looked worried. 'But we are going home to Glasgow tomorrow,' she said.

'Don't worry,' said Sheila. 'I've got your number and I'll

be in touch. If the panel agrees with us, they might want to interview you.'

'Are you serious?' asked Emma, with some excitement.

'Of course I am,' said Sheila.

And then she was off, heading down the driveway while chatting to Colin.

The sun did not shine on the last day of the holiday. The sky was dark and rain threatened as the children tidied up. As always, Emma had a lot more to do than Ben as her things were spread around everywhere. While Emma hunted for a pair of earphones that had gone missing, Ben had time to examine the old lists he had composed before even starting out on this trip. The whole holiday had been much more interesting than he could have imagined – and that was without Colin's boat. In fact, as he sat there thinking about his time in Achnabreck, he realised that he hadn't done any fishing, not even with his Dad.

When Emma was finally ready, they both walked up to Colin's to see him for the last time. After they had been supplied with chocolate biscuits, they asked him to tell them all he knew about the legend of Fiachra and Mor. The tale took a while, but Colin was a born storyteller. By the time he had finished describing Fiachra's duel with Ketil, it was time for them to head back to their Aunt's cottage.

They could hear the boot of Katie's car slamming shut as their parents finished loading up for the journey home. Because they now had two cars, Ben and Emma would be travelling separately. 'I don't have time to tell you much more now,' Colin said, looking down at his watch.

'But what happened to Conall?' asked Ben. 'Did Fiachra fight another duel with him?'

'No, he didn't,' said Colin. 'After Ketil had been killed and the Vikings all left the district, Fiachra was a hero. And Conall realised that Mor was not interested in him. So he left Dunadd.'

Ben looked disappointed. 'What about Gris?'

Colin shrugged. 'He was never heard of again either.'

'And Legbiter?' asked Emma.

'What do you mean *and Legbiter*?'

'Do you think the story of the sword could be true?'

'We know for a fact that it *is* true,' said Colin. 'Magnus Barefoot was a real person and he *was* killed in Ireland. He really did have a sword called Legbiter, and when he died, some of his troops brought the sword back to Norway.'

Emma spoke again. 'Did Fiachra and Mor ever get married?'

'They surely did,' replied Colin. 'And their marriage was a very happy one. They settled in Asknish. Unfortunately, they didn't have any children and Mor died quite young, when an illness spread to the villages on the coast. Quite a few people in Asknish died from this illness, and Fiachra was devastated. He loved Mor so much he couldn't bear to be parted from her. The legend says that he also died young – of a broken heart.'

Emma frowned. 'Can that be true? Is it possible to die of a broken heart?'

'Who knows?' Colin shrugged. 'Who knows if any part of a legend is true? But if your discovery is as exciting as I think it is, then some parts of this particular legend must be true.' The big man stood up and crossed to the door. 'It's been great seeing you. I look forward to catching up with you both next time you're here. And I'm sorry I don't have the boat anymore.'

Cameron's voice was calling them down to the cars where Aunt Isobel was standing to wave them off. But Ben wasn't finished. 'What about fighting? You've been telling us about a seventeen-year old boy. If Fiachra was a great hero at that age, did he fight more battles when he was grown up?'

Colin smiled down at Ben. 'He certainly did. In later years, Fiachra again had to protect the country from the Norsemen, and he fought for freedom by the side of Somerled. In fact, he was one of the senior officers in Somerled's army.'

Emma looked up. 'Who is Somerled?'

Colin ruffled her hair with his hand.

'Och, lassie, that's another story for another day!'

THE STONE

It was a bitterly cold afternoon, and the climber stopped to wind his cloak more tightly around him as protection against the fierce and icy wind. The further he ascended the slope, the more he marvelled that Breccan could still make this journey on his old legs.

The cell had come into view and he knew that the monk was there, protected from the cold, wind and rain. The building was small but practical and though the priest continued to serve the people of the surrounding glens, he still loved the times when he could be back on his hill, able to read, write and contemplate.

As the man approached the place of prayer, he took a moment to take in his surroundings. On top of the ridge, the wind was at its strongest and he had to plant his footsteps firmly to steady his balance. The view was partly obscured by clouds, but he had been here before often enough to know what it *could* be like. The whole world was spread out before him and this hill was the one place where it could all be seen – this place that was so near to heaven above.

When the knock came, the old man was taken by surprise. Visitors here were scarce. As he pulled back the door and the wind swept into the small room, Breccan peered ahead, his eyes trying to adjust to a different kind of light. 'Fergus, how are you?' he asked, when he recognised the face beneath the hood.

'I am well, Father,' said the stone cutter, 'though I fear I'm getting a bit old for this climb!'

'Come in, come in, out of the cold,' said Breccan.

As Breccan pushed the door shut, Fergus sat down at the far wall. There was barely room for two men to sit together in that small space. Fergus felt awkward for a moment. He had a feeling that he had interrupted a deep silence; as Breccan settled down across from him, the monk didn't speak for some time, as if he were trying to finish his meditation.

When Breccan did finally open his mouth, it was only to remark on the weather outside.

'At least it is warm and dry in here,' said Fergus.

'I have you to thank for that,' said Breccan. 'You have built this place so well. I will always be grateful to you.'

'You picked a great place for me to build,' said Fergus. 'From here you can see the whole world. Step outside of this cell and you can see everything.'

Breccan smiled over at his old friend. 'I prefer to step *inside* and look at another world – the world of my inner life,' he said.

Fergus looked around him. There was so little to see: a couple of candles, some parchments, writing materials, and the simple mat where the old man slept.

'How are you, Fergus?' Breccan had asked the question before, but it seemed as if he was looking for a different answer. 'What brings you here today?'

Fergus looked down to the earth floor for a few moments before making his reply. 'I'm still feeling sad about Fiachra.'

Breccan nodded. 'It's only been three weeks since we buried him at St Bride's Chapel. It's no surprise. We all miss him.'

'When the sickness came to the loch and Mor died, it was a tragedy. But I never believed that I would outlive both of them.'

'Nor me,' said Breccan. 'And I'm a good bit older than you.'

Fergus spoke again. 'You know, I think that we have something in common. Over the years, I think that we were both closer to him than anyone else.'

'I think Mor might want to argue that!'

'Apart from Mor!' Fergus agreed. 'But he really loved you, Breccan. And I know he and I were close too, especially when he came to the crannog to help me with my work.'

'How *is* your work?'

'It's been going well. I've just finished the building repairs at Dunadd. And that's what brought me here today.'

Breccan looked puzzled.

'I have a good piece of smooth stone left over from the work,' said Fergus, 'and I wanted to do something with it – something that might preserve the memory of Fiachra.'

'What are you thinking of?'

'I want to put something on the stone but I need your help. Can you show me how to make the word?' Fergus pointed over to the parchments in the corner. 'I want to carve his name but I do not know how to make it. I cannot write things as you can. I want to make his name on the stone and bring it up here beside your cell, so people will always remember the debt we owe to this man. From here, Fiachra can stand guard over our shores, and inspire us to defend ourselves.'

'Listen, Fiachra is dead now, Fergus. He is safely with God.'

'But his soul or his angel might still be here to help us. God might send his angel to protect us. Fiachra was a good man. Do you not believe that God could use his spirit for a good cause even after death? You have told us often before now that death has been defeated.'

Breccan smiled at Fergus. He didn't want to argue, so he reached forwards and gently laid a hand on Fergus' shoulder. 'Very well, I will write the word and you can carve it onto the stone. But I think there should be more than one word. If Fiachra is to be here on this hill I am sure he would want Mor to be with him. Fiachra was never complete without Mor.'

'You are right, as usual,' said Fergus. 'I will do that. I will make Mor on the stone if you show me how. And this way, we will always remember them: Fiachra and Mor.'

HISTORICAL NOTE

Magnus Olafsson (also as known as Barefoot) was crowned King Magnus III of Norway in 1093 after the death of his father. His cousin Haakon Magnusson refused to accept his rule, and for two years until Haakon's death there were two rival kings.

When Magnus became undisputed ruler of the country, he spent much of his reign seeking to increase Norse control, carrying out military campaigns in Scotland, Wales, Ireland, and Sweden. King Edgar of Scotland offered to give Magnus control of all Scottish islands in exchange for peace. Magnus readily agreed, and in 1098 he had his longship dragged across the isthmus at Tarbert, thus laying claim to the peninsula of Kintyre as an 'island.'

Magnus was killed in an ambush while fighting in Ireland in 1103 near Downpatrick. Although his body was never recovered, his remaining followers took up his famous sword *Legbiter* and returned it to Norway.

Legbiter had an ivory hilt and a handgrip wound with gold thread.

Magnus was the last Norwegian King to die on foreign soil.